Joseph's Story

Shawn Darren Stanley

Joseph's Story

Copyright © 2011 by Shawn Darren Stanley

ISBN (978-0-615-56760-0)

Printed in USA by 48HrBooks

Dedication

A special dedication to my wife, the one and only, Stephanie Stanley for helping me follow my dreams.

I also dedicate this book to my children. Riess, Rhett, Sierra, Ethan, Makenzie and Brielle.

My Wife and family are my most wonderful dream come true.

Introduction

"Follow your dreams, fore when you do, it's amazing how many come true."

I got the idea for this book right before Christmas-2010. During this time, like all Christmas seasons in the past, we took time to celebrate our Savior's birth and to emphasize certain elements of the Christmas story. As I contemplated the story as a whole, I began to be curious about what Joseph went through at the beginning of his life with Mary. Joseph was a man of clear understanding and a follower of the Law of Moses, which must have caused an internal conflict for him when learning of Mary's impending pregnancy.

As I became more and more immersed in this story, I tried to comprehend what manner of man Joseph must have been. I came to believe that, along with Mary, Joseph was chosen from the beginning; foreordained to be the proxy of the Almighty God unto raising Jesus, on this earth. How daunted I would feel if I were asked to do this, to be the earthly father to the Only Begotten Son, – how inadequate and unworthy I would feel. What manner of man would be worthy of such a task and honor? Joseph would have to be of similar character, faith, love, integrity, and courage to that of God. He had to have the implicit trust of our

Heavenly Father, for no righteous father would give up care of his child unless he knew what kind of person he was leaving him with. After coming to this understanding, I wanted to show circumstances in the story that illustrate the characteristics that Joseph must have possessed. I believe Joseph was a wonderful man and one that we could all learn from and strive to emulate. It is too bad that we do not have more writings about Joseph.

Joseph's spirituality, mannerisms, character, principles, values and morals must have played an integral part in the young Savior's life. Joseph would have taught the value of work, the importance of obedience and sacrifice, kindness and charity – all the things that would have shaped Jesus in his formative years. These things would have stayed with him throughout his life and ministry.

We don't know a lot about Joseph, his family, the circumstances surrounding his hearing the news of Mary's pregnancy, his wedding, and his preparation for the birth of the Savior. These thoughts kept occupying my mind and I found myself pondering them more and more. I thought of the love that Joseph must have had for Mary and what he must have gone through to bring the Savior into this world.

In my research, I reviewed many sources, some merely legends, to find out more about the places, histories, travel, traditions, and ceremonies of Joseph and Mary's time and culture as well as those of Mary and Joseph themselves. One legend I found said that Joseph might have died when the Savior was around 19 years old. If this were true then the Savior would have automatically taken over as provider

5

and guardian for his mother and siblings. This may be why the Savior, in his ministry, had so much compassion for the widows and the fatherless – because he knew firsthand the struggles they endured. He showed the same compassion even on his last day in mortality when he turned the care of his mother over to one of his disciples by saying in John 19:26-27 "…Mother, behold thy son! Then saith he to the disciple, Behold Thy Mother! And from that hour that disciple took her unto his own home."

I believe the story of Mary and Joseph would have been a great love story, one that has been hidden by the ages. So I thought I would embark on writing a novel of historical fiction based on the events that we know of. This was a lot harder than I originally thought. And it was tough to try to get the feel for what life could have been like in Nazareth at that time.

While I make no claim of accuracy to the historical authenticity of many elements of the story such as the hierarchy of the Roman military or the location of King Herod in regards to the region I did want the Lord to approve of my attempt, and I prayed that I would be guided in the more important parts of the story.

I have taken incredible liberties with some facets of the tale in order to make the story exciting while bringing actual events and circumstances into it. I have added chapter notes at the end of the book to show where some of the elements came from and what the events in the story were based on. These may help bring this story more to life for the reader and give additional insight into the life of

Joseph and the vital necessity of the birth, life, ministry and atonement of our Savior – the creator and the finisher of our faith and our only hope to return to our heavenly home.

So enjoy Joseph's story, a traditional story come to life from his perspective.

Preface

You could cut the excitement with a knife. The pen had just been handed to Joseph, he looked at the document. All eyes were on him.

After signing, he and Mary would be betrothed. His eyes rose from the document to look at Mary. She was beaming with her hands folded up under her chin with anticipation.

Joseph again looked at the document and with a smile on his face signed his name and it was done.

There was an eruption of cheering and celebration. The reception celebration that followed was incredible. The food and dancing were second to none. Everyone was having a wonderful time and why not, this was a very joyous occasion.

Joseph was the happiest man alive. He was going to marry the most beautiful girl in Nazareth. He had some of the best friends anyone could want.

His carpentry business was taking off. His furniture and other products that he had built were the talk of the town.

Everything seemed to be going Joseph's way. He had his whole life planned out. Then it all changed.

Chapter One

"Is it true? It can't be," he thought. "How could she do this to me? What about our marriage plans? I don't know what to do. I feel numb. Numb but angry… yet I still love her. I feel like my heart is about to break. What will my mother and father think? What about my friends? Where did I fail her?"

Joseph snapped out of his self-indulgent trance realizing he was emerging from an obscure alley into the main market area just in time to see a Roman soldier riding fast on his horse coming straight for him. Joseph – trying to dive out of the way – slipped and fell on the street. With no time to regain his footing, he instinctively curled up and covered his head, waiting for the impending trampling. The horse let out a frightening sound; dug in all four hooves, sunk down on his rear to the ground and started to slide. Just inches short of Joseph the horse was able to gain control and reared almost straight up, letting out another frightened neigh, nearly throwing his rider. The soldier – yelling and wrenching back on the reins – lost the struggle to keep his balance and started sliding off the side of the horse. Trying to right himself, the Roman made one last attempt to yank harder on the reins, which now were supporting his full weight on the animal's neck making the horse turn slightly to the left before his hooves came crashing down right next to Joseph's head.

The jolt of the horse's hooves hitting the ground was all that it took and the soldier came off the horse and crashed onto the street. Rolling to his feet, he immediately ran over and started yelling at Joseph. "You stupid Jew, if my horse hadn't stopped I would have gladly trampled over you. I should have you arrested and flogged for impeding the travel of a Roman soldier. But I am late to deliver information to Herod." After threatening a kick toward Joseph, he spit on the ground in Joseph's direction. Then the Roman got back on his horse and was off.

Joseph was still in shock from what had just happened. He didn't even remember any of the words the soldier had said to him. All Joseph knew was that he was lucky to be alive. Joseph was large in stature and had a well-developed body from his work in the trade of building and carpentry, he stood just short of 6 feet tall and looked quite intimidating. However, he was a very passive person and easy to be around. He was good with tools and well-coordinated. He was extremely witty and to the amazement of his friends and family was able to solve any puzzle given him. He was also clever in negotiating, which came in very handy when dealing with customers. Joseph was a direct descendant of King David and if it were not for the Roman empire, Joseph would be next in line to be king of Judea.

The Romans soldiers treated Jews mostly with disdain and they seemed disheartened to be assigned to serve their empire in Galilee and the surrounding people with their strange, one God, one religion. The region of Galilee was not considered the most glorious place for a proud Roman to serve in the imperial army, but there were some perks.

The region was a long way away from the emperor and because of that distance certain indiscretions were overlooked and over time had become commonplace. Looting a home and keeping the spoils if a family were unable to pay taxes for example; paying taxes was a nicer way of saying extortion and robbery. If a family was not able to pay the high taxes due to Rome, then Roman soldiers, under the command of a centurion, could legally confiscate that family's possessions – including their home – arrest them, and take them to Rome to be sold as slaves. The wealthy were often targeted not just because they had more to give, but because Roman authorities feared that if people were allowed to gather more wealth they may be more likely to fund and support rebellions. So, often wealthy families were treated harshly.

Corruption was rampant in the upper levels of governments as well. At times, government officials would pretend to show leniency to families and pardon them from the responsibility of paying their full tax, only to turn them over to the centurion and his soldiers later on. Then in return for turning a family in, those officials would get a cut of the confiscated property because of their effort to collect past due taxes.

"Joseph, are you alright?" Amos, Joseph's long time friend and colleague came running over to him, grabbing his arm to help him to his feet. "I'm alright, Amos, thank you for your help and kindness," responded Joseph, his voice still shaky from the incident. Others on the street who had stopped their activities to watch the excitement unfold went back to their day as if nothing had happened. Even though most Jews hated the way they were treated under Roman rule there was nothing they could do about it at the moment. Acting out would just bring down the full might of the Roman military on all Jews.

"Someday those Roman soldiers will get what is coming to them," yelled Amos in the direction of the departing soldier. "When our prophesied king comes he will avenge us." Amos said in disgust.

"Amos", said Joseph, "I need to find Mary. Have you seen her?" Amos lowered his head. He knew why Joseph was looking for his espoused wife. "I have not seen her. Joseph, I have to tell you. Mary's friend Nalla, told me about Mary and asked that I look for you. I am afraid that it won't be long before more people hear of this also. Is it true, is Mary pregnant?" Amos could see the pain in Joseph's eyes. They both knew the ramifications according to Jewish law if indeed she was found to be pregnant outside of their betrothal. After a betrothal, a couple was given a waiting period of 12 months before the official 'home taking' was allowed. This ensured that the betrothal hadn't been made in order to cover up an illegitimate pregnancy or a pregnancy resulting from a rape by a

Roman soldier – a situation which was becoming more and more common.

Joseph, being an upright man, a man of integrity, clear understanding, and one who followed the Law of Moses closely, knew what could become of his lovely fiancée and her child in this circumstance. A baby born out of wedlock was considered a bastard and would be unable to marry any legitimate Jew when old enough. Right, wrong or indifferent, it was a fact that the children of unwed or unfaithful parents became victims and bore the burden of his or her parents' sin.

Luckily, the law had become less strict since the days of Moses and a little more tolerance was being allowed on some levels, including divorce.

"Joseph, what are you going to do if this is true?" asked Amos.

"I don't even want to think about that right now," Joseph replied. "I just want to find Mary and talk to her."

Joseph, however, had already gone through his options in his mind. He could just leave and abandon Mary, bringing fines of property and shame upon himself and his family. He could turn her over to the authorities. After which, upon finding her guilty, they would stone her. He could divorce her – a proceeding which would not be quiet and would require two witnesses to finalize. Public shame would follow her because everyone would think she was unfaithful and the cause of the divorce. Or he could forgive her of her transgression, allow her to come into his home and adopt her child as his own.

If he found the rumors of her pregnancy to be true, Joseph wanted to be able to forgive her and continue with their wedding, but the shame and jealousy at the thought of her being with another man seemed a hurdle he was uncertain he could get over. "How could I, a descendant of King David, allow a bastard child into my bloodline?" Joseph thought to himself. Under the current Roman rule, Joseph's ancestry did not carry much weight, but maintaining his Jewish royal heritage was important to him.

Another question sprang into his mind, "Would I be able to raise it as my own?" He did not know if he was capable of such a task. "Too much dwelling on the negative," Joseph thought. "I don't even know yet if this rumor is true."

Amos, seeing Joseph drifting off into his mental deliberation, tried to cheer him up. "Joseph, I am your friend. You can count on that friendship to continue. I will speak with my father Zebediah to see if the law could be sensitive to you and Mary. Having friends with fathers in politics has its benefits," he said. "In the meantime you should go home and ask your father if he has heard from her."

"Thanks Amos for your friendship," Joseph responded. "It means a lot to me. I must go and keep searching for Mary."

The sun was close to midday. It was hotter than usual in Nazareth for this time of year. The earth was cracked, yearning to soak up any moisture that would come. But nothing appeared to quench its thirst anytime soon. There was not a cloud to be seen. The sun was the only object in the sky. Joseph didn't even seem to notice the heat. Agony and anger started to fill Joseph's mind at the same time. Anger grew in the pit of his stomach and Joseph was surprised at his thoughts and scared to think what he might be capable of in his current state.

Trying to shake out of his slump he began whispering to himself, "Where could she be? I have searched everywhere I can think of." Then the thought occurred to him, "What if she has been looking for me? Maybe Amos was right. I will go to my father's house and see if he has seen her."

Chapter Two

Gaius, the head communications courier to the local government raced to the gate of the residence of Herod, King of Judea, stopping only to present his authorization papers to the guards. His visit with Herod was urgent – precious minutes were wasted plus the embarrassment of falling off his horse to avoid trampling a lowly Jew – running late only exacerbated his urgency. After seeing the urgency of his visit, the guards quickly opened the large black iron gate and the horse bolted again at top speed up the well-groomed path leading to the front door of his Excellency.

The house guards noticing Gaius's approach ran out to accept his horse and direct him to where he could find the king. "He has been expecting you and your report," the head guard told him. "He asked that you hurry." Gaius ran at top speed through large front doors, across the smooth white marble floors and out the back door onto the splendid and vast patio where Herod sat at a large dark wooded table. The table formed a perfect circle, had thick sturdy legs, and the crest of the Roman Eagle exquisitely carved into its top as a symbol of the serious business that was to take place with any assembly gathered around it. The table had been given to him by a Roman general. Seated at the round table with Herod were several of his councilors and war strategists. Gaius could see plans and strategies were well on the way judging by the scrolls of drawings, various attack plans and designs of the surrounding cities spread all over the table.

Even though Herod was supposedly a Jewish King, he realized where his true allegiance lay and that Rome allowed him to be king to appease the Jews with the idea that they had their own ruler. Although Rome had given him autonomy, he knew where the true power lay.

"I say we crush them before they have a chance to strike. This will keep casualties to a minimum," said Gnaeus, member of the council.

Gaius came running down the stairs into the patio area. As soon as Gaius approached, the heated conversation around the table ceased. All eyes were glued to Gaius. Herod wasted no time. "What is your report, Gaius?"

"Your Excellency," Gaius said, giving the customary Roman salute. "Our spies have confirmed that the Zealots are organizing, and plans for a major revolt are imminent."

Voices erupted from around the table, fingers were pointing and accusatory words flew back and forth louder than the screams from the stadium during a chariot race. "Silence," yelled Herod. All voices immediately stopped. The buzzing of bees on the flowering bush next to the water fountain was the only sound. "We will not regain order with these Jews while we are fighting amongst ourselves," Herod said.

"Gaius, what seems to be the reason for their revolt?" asked Herod.

"The Jews take offense at giving their allegiance to Roman banners which display an image of Caesar. They believe swearing such an oath before such a banner would be against their law of worshipping graven images and would bring condemnation from their God. They asked that we take the banners down. Upon our refusal to do so, the gathering of the Zealots and plans of revolt began," responded Gaius.

There were a few moments of silence and then Herod spoke. "Gentlemen and defenders of Rome and Judea, the Zealots believe that by showing their bravery, their God will reward them – not only with victory against Rome – but victory in their heaven as well. They also believe in a prophecy, which they think will happen soon. It foretells the royal birth of a new Jewish king -- capable of delivering them from the boundaries of the current Jewish government and the Roman empire. This has given them an extra source of courage.

"There is no doubt that our soldiers will be able to put down this rebellion, but at what cost?" Herod paused. "Chances for casualties on both sides are high. Fighting and beating the Jews in a religious confrontation will only bring future uprisings.

"The best way to win this particular war is not to fight it with force, but with stratagems and cunning. Herod started to bark orders to those in council around the table. Aulus, we have been padding the pockets of the son of a Jewish politician, Amos, son of Zebediah. He has been tasked with infiltrating the Zealot movement. I have asked him to become one of them and gain their trust. I think it is time to utilize his efforts. Have Amos call a meeting with the Zealots, convincing them to hold off their revolt for a time until sufficient funds can be gathered together in his care. Have him arrange for the money from all the members and those sensitive to their cause to flow to his estate. Tell Amos that for his help five percent of the spoils will be his."

Quintus, send a message to Pontius Pilate alerting him of our plan and that we will give him word after all the money is collected. We can then declare Amos a traitor, kill him and confiscate all his property. By so doing we will keep 10 percent of the spoils and the rest will be sent to Rome.

"I want to conclude this plan in 8 months' time and tie it into Rome's plans to conduct a census and tax of all

17

subjects of Rome. If we conclude our plan during this timeframe the Zealots will be required to go to their home cities. Thus dividing them up and not allowing them to congregate to form new plans.

"Herod," said Marcus, another member of the council. "What a magnificent plan. It will put an end to the funding of our Jewish foes, crush their fervor for their cause, and bring a fortune into our coffers without endangering any of our own...Brilliant.

"Does anyone in my council oppose this plan?" Herod asked. "Good. Then it is unanimous. Make it so. Thank you Gaius for your report. You are all free to go."

Chapter Three

By the time Joseph reached his father's home, the sun was low in the sky and its direct heat was subsiding. The sun appeared larger than normal. It was a beautiful dark orange color and looked heavy as it began its slow descent below the horizon.

Joseph was glad to be close to his childhood home. He was dehydrated, his feet needed attention from the journey and he was in need of nourishment. He hadn't seen his father, Jacob, since his betrothal reception months ago. His engagement. He remembered the happiness of that day. He had felt he was the luckiest Jew alive. Mary was the prettiest girl that he had ever seen and she was going to be his wife. His happiness was all-consuming when they both signed the *ketubah* (marriage contract) which made their relationship binding by Jewish law and from that point it made him smile each time he was able to call her his wife even though the ceremony had still been 12 months away at that point.

His thoughts snapped back to the present. All that may be in jeopardy now as remembrance of her pregnancy brought him back to his seemingly depressing reality. "I thought she was happy," he thought. "I saw the look in her eyes when our parents announced their agreement to our engagement. She *was* happy. I could see it. What happened since then?"

Jacob, Joseph's father saw Joseph approaching and alerted Joseph's mother Sarah and asked that she prepare some water for him. Jacob then opened the door and quickly went out to greet him. Joseph saw his father and quickened his pace to meet him. They met with an embrace. "Son, I have missed your company and so has your mother." Joseph didn't reply but Jacob could see concern in his son's eyes and so he said, "Come inside, wash your feet, and get some nourishment. We can talk then." Joseph was relieved that he didn't have to explain the reasons for his visit so soon after arriving.

Stepping inside the cool darkness of his father's home was a welcome relief from the heat. He and Jacob sat down by the dining table. "Here Joseph," his mother said, handing him a cup of water and placing a bowl of water at his feet for so he could wash up.

"Thank you Mother," Joseph said. "I have forgotten the benefits of being home."

"You're welcome son," his mother replied, giving him a loving grin. "I have some food prepared. I will get some for you." Joseph was grateful to have such caring and loving parents.

Joseph's father, Jacob, had built quite an import business and was doing well for himself, but seemed to remain humble and grounded, content with living a simple life. His home was modest in size and did not show his real wealth. But it made him happy to use a portion of his means in helping others and in giving tithes and offerings.

Jacob had a long salt and pepper colored beard. You could see he had had a plentiful number of life experiences by the wrinkles and lines in his face and hands. He seemed to stick with black and white clothes while Joseph's mother wore more colorful attire. She always said she wore colors so she could stand out next to such a handsome husband. They made a very handsome couple – a couple whose marriage had been long and happy.

Joseph only aspired to have a marriage like his parents -- a marriage where each partner always showed love and compassion for the other no matter what the consequences.

"Joseph, how is your carpentry business going?" Jacob asked, trying to start a conversation with small talk. "I have been hearing around Nazareth that your furniture is becoming the best in town." Joseph seemed to light up with this compliment from his father.

"Yes, my business is doing very well," he said. "I have back orders lined up. But I have still found time to finish the *huppah* (marriage canopy) for the wedding." Joseph's smile quickly turned to a blank stare as he realized that there may be no use for the huppah after that day.

The huppah is a portable canopy a couple would stand under during a wedding ceremony. The ceremony was frequently conducted in the late afternoon or in the evening under the stars. The stars were especially symbolic since they related to the blessing given by God to the Patriarch Abraham that his children shall be "as the stars of the heavens."

"Joseph," Jacob started," I wanted to talk--"

"Have you heard from Mary?" Joseph interrupted with an anxious tone in his voice, not being able to hold in the real reason for his visit.

"Why yes son, we have," Jacob hesitantly responded.

"What did she say?" said a surprised Joseph.

"Son, she sent a courier for us and you. In her note to us she said that she needed to speak to you, face to face, but did not know how to approach you yet." Joseph's face turned to anguish and his head fell into his hands. Joseph was surprised to feel his eyes welling with tears.

"Joseph, she also left a letter for you." Jacob reached into his side pouch and pulled out a parchment neatly folded and sealed. Joseph looked up and saw the parchment in Jacob's outstretched hand. "Go. Read it in private. But when you're finished please will you let us know what all of this means?" Jacob asked.

Joseph quickly regained his composure; acted as if he was rubbing the tiredness out of his eyes and slowly reached for the letter and took it from his father's hands. He then retired to the bench in the back garden as the sun continued its descent into the night, and read the letter. Unknown to him, his parents were looking to see if they could get some clue by his reaction as to what Mary was telling their son. Whatever it was, they knew that it was tearing Joseph apart. Joseph opened the letter and began to read.

Dear Joseph,

I am sorry I am not there with you in person. I desperately need to see you and tell you so much, but I am afraid that you may not believe what is happening to me. So much has happened in the last few days that I don't know where to begin. I want to see you so much, have you hold me in your arms and let me know that everything is going to be alright. I am scared Joseph, and I don't know what is to become of me.

Please don't think ill of me and know that my love for you is endless. I can't bring myself to tell you everything in this letter. It deserves to be spoken of in person. I am afraid my fear has got the best of me – and not knowing who else to turn to – I have left to visit my cousin Elisabeth in Hebron who is expecting a child, even in her old age. When you get this letter I will have already left. Please don't worry, I have made safe travel plans and will contact you shortly.

Love, Mary

As a tear rolled down Joseph's cheek his feelings were a jumble of confusion. He wanted to feel relieved that her love for him was intact, but her not being able to tell him troubling news made him fear the reports of her pregnancy might be true. Wiping his eyes, he stood up and quickly turned around to see his parents acting as if they were being attentive to other things rather than spying on him. This didn't make him upset because he knew of their concern for him.

His walk was slow, but thoughtful back to the house. He opened the back door and saw his mother and father looking at him. Jacob stood behind Sarah in an archway of the dining room with his hands on Sarah's shoulders. They didn't have to speak. Joseph knew their question by looking at their faces. As he opened his mouth, to his surprise, the news that he had been holding in for so long came tumbling out. "I have heard gossip that Mary may be pregnant." Sarah's hand came up to cover her mouth to mask her obvious shock.

"Son, do you know this to be true?" asked Jacob.

"I don't. This is why I am trying to find her – to ask in person," Joseph replied.

"You wouldn't be able to speak with her alone without a chaperone anyway," Jacob said.

"All our attention to tradition and ceremonial rituals will not hold any merit if what I have heard today is true," snapped Joseph. Joseph's parents' expressions lightened somewhat knowing what their son said made sense.

"In the letter Mary wrote, she spoke of her love for me and that she is scared and has left to travel to Hebron to visit her cousin Elisabeth," continued Joseph.

"Hebron?" Sarah spoke up, "That is so far away and not a journey that can be taken lightly. Jacob, we must stop her."

"She is already gone, mother. She told me in her letter that by the time I read her words she would have already left. She did say that she had made safe travel arrangements," mumbled Joseph. "I must travel to Hebron and speak with her."

Joseph tried to walk past his parents to go back into the dining room, but Jacob left his wife's side and blocked his son's path. He placed a hand on Joseph's shoulder, then lifted Joseph's chin to be able to look him in the eye and asked, "If you find this rumor to be true, what are you prepared to do?"

Staring back into the familiar face of his father, Joseph replied, "I'm not sure, I haven't thought it through that far."

"Certainly you cannot continue with your wedding plans," his father said. "This would not be wise – our family name and reputation would be damaged considerably. It would affect both your business and mine when customers found out you were raising a bastard child." Jacob finished.

The shock on Joseph's face was obvious. He shrugged off his father's hands and stumbled a couple steps back. Realizing that what his father said was true, he fell back into a chair. Agony was etched into his expression. He rubbed his face with his hands as if to wipe emotion away. And trying to add clarity to the situation, he said, "If this is found to be true I will prepare a divorce from our wedding contract, but it will be in private. I do not want her to be humiliated."

A divorce from a wedding contract would take the signatures of two witnesses. This would be as private as a divorce could be. After the groom has the divorce decree signed the woman would no longer have access to the groom or the groom's family. If the bride turned out to be pregnant everyone would think that infidelity was the cause for the divorce and she would more than likely be shunned – not by law – but by the social system that was in place at the time. She would have a very difficult time finding someone to marry and her child would never be accepted as a full Jew.

"It is settled then," spoke Jacob, "I will await your word when you come back from Hebron and then make proper arrangements."

Pain started to show again in Joseph's expression. It was all moving too fast. "She loves me. She wrote it in the letter. She's scared and alone," Joseph thought to himself.

Joseph's mother interrupted his thoughts. "Joseph, please stay here for a time, we can help you prepare provisions for such a journey, make proper business arrangements for your absence and check on when the next caravan will be traveling to Jerusalem."

"I will not need a caravan, Mother, because I will travel through Samaria," Joseph replied.

"Joseph, think clearly. It will not do you or Mary any good if you get killed on the way to see her. It is not safe and it is unwise. Besides Samaritans are unclean," Jacob answered.

"Samaritans are only unclean because we decided that they are unclean," Joseph said. "Their religion is not much different from ours. Yet we hate each other because we can't accept the other group's beliefs. I do not understand how the fact that a person worships the God of Israel a little differently than we do makes them unclean." Joseph rubbed his face with his hands again trying to ground his thoughts better.

"This endless hatred between us does make travel in their land unsafe," Jacob persisted.

"Maybe my plan is rash but I want to see her sooner than later. Every day between now and then will only eat at me more and more," Joseph said in distress.

Sarah walked over, knelt down, took Joseph's hand and said, "Son, you need to rest. Let us eat some dinner and then let our sleep help make more sense of today's events. Tomorrow your thoughts will be more practical."

"Thank you, Mother, I would like that. I love both of you."

"We love you too son," his mother and father replied, almost in unison.

Chapter Four

Mary was traveling to her cousin, Elisabeth's home in the hillside country of Hebron. The day's travel was almost over. She had just eaten the last piece of bread she had packed for that day's portion of the journey. The road was dusty and her throat was dry. Tonight she would be able to fill her canteen and drink till she was content.

It had been a few days since an angel named Gabriel had visited her in her garden. Excitement and fear had captured her whole being. Still not able to fully comprehend the angelic event, even now it continued to play over and over in her mind. "I am the one, the one chosen to be the mother of the Messiah! Is it so? it must be. Gabriel said it," she thought to herself Her mind still reeled from the experience, going back and forth from excitement to fear. Excited to be in such favor in the eyes of the Lord, looking forward with great eagerness and anxiety to her expected pregnancy and fear for how she was to explain this to Joseph. She felt alone in this respect.

She didn't really care what others would think of her right now, except for Joseph, her betrothed husband. Tt bothered her deeply to think of how he would react to this news. "Will he be able to believe that I am still faithful to him and that this is a pregnancy from heaven?" Hearing herself explain it made her realize how outlandish it sounded. She didn't think she herself would believe this story coming from another if she hadn't experienced it herself. Her letter to Joseph was short, but she didn't know what to say, except that she loved him and that everything would be explained later.

Mary was unaware that Joseph had already heard that she might be pregnant. She had only told one friend of her angelic visit because she felt that if she didn't tell someone she would explode. Her thoughts were all she had while traveling in a large caravan towards Jerusalem. A caravan was the only safe way to travel such a distance. Mary felt safe in this particular caravan since it consisted of over 100 men and soldiers all traveling to Jerusalem for an annual festival. They were in the fourth day of their 10-day journey from Nazareth to Jerusalem. They were safely going down the Roman road through the Jericho valley and making very good time.

As subjects of Rome, access to the well-built roads and other industrious works of the Roman builders was one positive thing that had come to the Jewish nation out of oppressive Roman rule. Most men walked the entire distance. But Mary traveled on a donkey; as was customary for women on a trip of such magnitude.

Two days were added to the caravan's journey by the need to go around Samaria instead of through it. Due to the hatred between Jews and Samaritans, travel through Samaria was very unsafe and Samaritan inn keepers would close their establishments to any Jews needing rest for the night. Therefore, travel from Nazareth would go eastward over steep terrain and then on a well trodden trail descending the other side of that steep area until the the caravan reached the Jericho River. After crossing on the east side of the river you could travel about 60 miles down the valley with mountains on both sides. This road was home to many thieves and extremely dangerous for any to travel alone, but in a large group or caravan safety was almost assured.

"Tomorrow," Mary thought, "we will be able to rest for a few days in Jericho. Then we can make the trek into the mountains of Jerusalem." She had no desire to speak with anyone traveling with her and being only sixteen years old her heart was heavy. She did not know where to turn for solace regarding the situation she found herself in. But because the angel had told her that Elisabeth was expecting a divine child as well, Mary thought that Elizabeth might understand better than most what she was going through. Therefore, she had decided to make the long trek of about 120 miles to visit her cousin. She also thought that she would be able to escape the awful looks and accusations of those in Nazareth after they found out about her pregnancy. In Hebron, she also would have time to think of a way to approach Joseph and pray that he would understand.

After staying with friends in Jerusalem for a time she would join another caravan traveling through Bethlehem and into Hebron. Although she would never be alone in her travel, she would be totally alone in spirit since she dared not speak of the things that were so burdensome to her heart. "Will he accuse me of adultery, abandon me? Will I have to carry this baby on my own? What is to become of this precious life that is beginning to grow within me?" Her worried thoughts continued until a mental prayer disrupted her depressed thoughts. "God, please hear the prayer of your servant. Thou knowest that I am willing to do thy will, no matter the cost. But if you will, have mercy on my situation and my dear espoused Joseph. Prepare him for the message of the coming of your son; that he may know of my devotion to thee and to him; that he may still take me in and have me as his wife and raise this child as his own." A surprising feeling of peace and comfort swept through her body. It felt as if her entire being was tingling. She felt as light as a feather and the depressing thoughts immediately left her mind – so much so that she knew the Lord was with her and that she was being watched over. Her countenance was relieved and her heart, much lighter.

Chapter Five

Joseph retired to sleep that night in the same room that he had grown up in. He still remembered when he was young and the time he had played with his father's scrolls –

something he was forbidden to do – and accidentally ripped one of them. He had taken the two ripped pieces into his room and tried to glue them back together with beeswax, honey, and tree sap; hoping that nobody would notice. Even though he had gotten in big trouble for disobeying his parents, those days were simpler and the problems of adults were the furthest considerations from his mind. Part of him wished he could go back to those young, simple days

Joseph prepared for bed and was surprised to realize how exhausted he felt. As soon as his head hit his pillow, he drifted into a deep sleep. Shortly after he was asleep, his mind started to wrestle with the day's events and became very disturbed.

During this time of unconscious distress a dream opened up to him. He dreamed a dream in which light filled the room where he slept making it brighter than noonday. Then an angel, dressed in a bright white robe, stood before his bed. The light seemed to be focused around the angel's body. Joseph noticed that the angel's feet did not touch the floor and appeared to be floating in the air. His feet were bare.

The angel introduced himself as Gabriel. "I don't understand," said a shocked Joseph. "I am a simple and humble man. For what reason is such a glorious being sent to speak with me?"

Gabriel's voice was soft and comforting as he said, "Joseph, thou son of David, fear not to take unto thee Mary thy wife: for that which is conceived in her is of the Holy Ghost. And she shall bring forth a son, and thou shalt call his name JESUS: for he shall save his people from their sins.

"Your calling is to provide for the child, rear him with correct values and principles and to help prepare him for his mission here on earth."

"How is this done, these happenings are mysterious unto me?" said Joseph. "Come with me," said Gabriel. Joseph was swept away in a vision to Mary's garden where he saw Gabriel speaking with Mary. Both of them were able to be spectators for this event in which he saw and heard the angel Gabriel speak these words to Mary.

"Hail, thou that art highly favored, the Lord is with thee: blessed art thou among women." Mary was startled and her hand rose close to her forehead as if to block out the brightness of the sun. She looked troubled and Gabriel continued. "Fear not, Mary: for thou hast found favor with God. And behold thou shalt conceive in thy womb, and bring forth a son, and shalt call his name Jesus. He shall be great, and shall be called the Son of the Highest: and the Lord God shall give unto him the throne of his father David:

"And he shall reign over the house of Jacob for ever; and of his kingdom there shall be no end."

Then said Mary unto the angel, "How shall this be, seeing I know not a man?"

And the angel answered and said unto her, "The Holy Ghost shall come upon thee, and the power of the Highest shall overshadow thee: therefore also that holy thing which shall be born of thee shall be called the Son of God." [3]

After seeing this, Joseph was immediately back in his room with Gabriel.

Joseph looked at Gabriel and asked with concern, "I am a humble man and do not feel worthy of this task and do not feel adequate to be in charge of such a divine and holy child. How will I be able to please God and raise his son?"

Gabriel responded, "You have been given all that thou needest to accomplish this and you can raise Jesus in a manner that your Father in Heaven would have him raised.

"Remember that Moses did not feel adequate to do the mighty work of bringing the children of Israel out of Egypt. Jeremiah felt unworthy and inadequate to be the prophet of the Lord to which the Lord responded,'"…Before I formed thee in the belly I knew thee; and before thou camest forth out of the womb I sanctified thee, and ordained thee a prophet unto the nations…. Thou shalt go to all that I shall send thee, and whatsoever I command thee thou shalt speak. Be not afraid of their faces: for I am with thee to deliver thee, saith the Lord.'"

Gabriel continued, "Joseph you are one like them, you were chosen before you were born and sanctified to raise the Only Begotten Son of God. Be not afraid for you will not be alone. You will have guidance, inspiration and revelation on how to raise the child.

"Joseph, I now covenant with you that if you are diligent in keeping Mary and her child safe from harm – that his birth may not be thwarted, even at the peril of your own life – I promise that you will have help from on high, from the heavens themselves, to aid you in this end.

"Joseph, believest thou the things which were shown to you?" Gabriel asked.

"You know I believe all your words," Joseph replied.

Gabriel then looked up into heaven and with a loud voice said, "Hosanna, to the Lord, the most High God and peace be upon you, Joseph, for believing in my words, If thou doest well you will be blessed from on high.

"Joseph awake now, and travel to Hebron where you will find Mary. She is frightened and does not know how to tell you about the baby. She is afraid that you will not marry her. Take care of her, provide for her, marry her and love her. Prepare all needful things for the birth of the child and you will be blessed."

Suddenly he was awake. The whole dream was fresh in his mind and he reflected on it again. He had been asked to raise the Son of God. The depth of this concept was just starting to hit him when he remembered the other parts of the dream. What a relief. His soul was rejoicing and excited over what him and Mary had been asked to do. He was also overjoyed to find out that Mary was still faithful to him and was highly favored of the Lord. He threw his hands in the air as a silent victory cheer, to keep from waking his parents.

Joseph lay back down but sleep had left him and he was as alert as at midday. He could tell that the anguish that showed on his face earlier had been replaced with a smile from ear to ear. Joseph stayed in his bed for only a minute. When he realized that he was not going to be able to go back to sleep he decided to get up and start to gather provisions for his journey to Hebron.

Chapter Six

Tiberius, the new centurion in the Galilee legion, had been recently transferred from Rome itself to oversee his first command. He opened the door of his modest quarters, stepped out and looked over his assigned garrison in the soldier courtyard. The darkness of the morning was still upon them. Long shadows stretched from the rising sun whose light would not be here for at least another 30 minutes. The soldiers were lined up in perfect order, ready for his command. Fifty additional men had been recently added to his garrison to help with tax collection. He wasn't sure why extra troops were ordered for this reason; collecting taxes was fairly routine. Unless of course, the tax collectors thought trouble might be probable while executing today's orders.

The Jews hated the idea that they were subjects of the Roman Empire. He could feel their evil stares every time he took his men down their streets. However, a local uprising would be foolish and would not halt tax collection activities. Lives would be lost, families destroyed and property confiscated. But he wouldn't put it past any Jew to be so foolish. The Jews seemed to be a very prideful people and any grudges seemed to be held close, never to be relinquished.

Tiberius was a proud, honorable soldier – proud to be in his current position to protect Rome in all its glory. However, he had a hard time understanding the religion of the local Jewish people. "Why just one God?" he asked himself. "Back in Rome I have 21 to choose from." Mars, the god of war, would help in battles; Neptune, the god of the sea to protect journeyers across the oceans; Minerva, the god of wisdom, to outsmart an opponent… just to name a few.

"It seems silly to trust all of your needs to just one deity," his thoughts continued.

Although Tiberius was proud to be a centurion – the position was what he had dreamed of attaining – it was with regret he learned that his main orders for some time were to ensure the safety and successful collection of taxes from certain wealthy families.

Tiberius, seeing the corruption in the local Roman government which pillaged the Jews of every bit it could cheat them out of; corruption among his comrades in arms who often spent time looting and falsely accusing Jews in order to take any of their possessions that the soldiers fancied; the corruption began to wear on him heavily. Innocent people, subjects of Rome, were being looked upon worse than the lowliest of slaves, tolerated only as a means to get gain. If this injustice didn't continue the Jews would be of no use for the empire. Any uprisings would be met with total destruction. This type of treatment of a people began to leave a bad taste in his mouth and he started to question the honor of being a Roman soldier.

"Centurion Tiberius, the men are awaiting their orders," remarked the garrison captain, Lucius.

"Thank you Lucius," answered Tiberius. They both embraced. This wasn't the first time that Lucius and Tiberius had met. They were long time childhood friends who had dreamed of being soldiers in the Roman military. They had gone through the ranks together and fought many battles side by side. Each had saved the life of the other on more than one occasion. They both valued each other's knowledge and expertise on war strategy, people, and reading situations. This was, however, the first time that one of them had outranked the other. This didn't seem to have an impact on their personal lives. But it did bother Lucius a little not being thought of as an equal to Tiberius and having to follow his explicit orders without question. Because of this power struggle, Lucius desperately wanted Tiberius to value his insight and not discount his input just because of his lower position.

In the Roman army a centurion would be approximately equal to the rank of a captain in the modern military.

"Men," Tiberius said, "today we are charged with the safe collection of past due taxes from three families in Nazareth: The households of Sadoc, son of Azor; Achim, son of Eliud; and Jacob, son of Matthan. We expect no surprises, but will need to be on guard at all times in case of any uprisings, whatever they may be. There will be no breaking of ranks without my explicit order. Any soldier to do so will be dealt with severely. We are Roman soldiers and will not dishonor our country by infringing on our own laws. If taxes are paid we will leave peacefully. That is all, be ready to march ten minutes from now. You're dismissed."

The men broke formation to head back to their barracks. With the morning exercises over, Lucius approached Tiberius with his concern. "Tiberius, these men are simple soldiers who are not paid very handsomely, and some not at all; taking property from these Jews is how they supplement their little income. Taking that option away from them may hamper their vigilance to their duties and may not prove wise."

"Lucius," Tiberius said, "if we can't trust our soldiers to be vigilant in their duties to the honor of their country, then we will discharge them and bring in other soldiers that will. I will not allow any breach in discipline under my command. These Jews – no matter how backwards their ways may be – are subjects of the Roman Empire and as long as they abide by our laws they will be treated as such. Is that understood?"

With hesitation and a little disturbance in his voice, Lucius said, "Yes, Sir, understood."

Chapter Seven

Joseph quickly started gathering provisions of all kinds for his journey to Hebron. It was early in the morning and the sun would rise shortly.

This journey was to be a joyous one when less than a day ago it had promised to be full of stress and worry. He did not realize how much commotion he was making until he looked up from scooping flour out of a barrel to see his mother and father, still in their sleeping clothes, looking perplexed, with tiredness in their eyes.

"Joseph, what on earth do you think you are doing?" asked his mother in a stern tone. Joseph froze in his tracks as he held a piece of morning bread in his mouth. After swallowing the bread, he blurted out in less than thirty seconds everything that had happened to him during the night.

"Mother, I had a vision in a dream where an angel of the Lord told me that Mary is carrying a child. But it is the son of God, which means she is still a virgin and I have been chosen to raise him as my own. She has remained faithful to me. I can still marry her! Isn't it great?" Joseph said in one breath, finishing with a childish, happy grin.

Jacob and Sarah both stood flabbergasted with their mouths hanging open as if they had just been struck by lightning. Both of them blinked their eyes rapidly trying to take in what they had just heard. Then both started talking at once but Jacob was the first to complete a remark, "What on earth....You're talking like a crazy person Joseph. Have you lost your mind?"

"You're telling me that you were told 'in a dream',"
Jacob said with emphasis, "that Mary's illegitimate child is
the prophesied Messiah, the Son of God?" he finished, not
sounding convinced.

"Hold on Father, I am neither crazy nor delusional."
Joseph's voice was a little calmer now, although he was
still in the heat of his excitement and was still beaming
with joy, with no sign of worry or doubt. "I need to take
more time to explain everything to you. Sit down and I will
explain better."

His mother and father were ushered to two chairs by an
enthusiastic Joseph. After they were seated, Joseph was met
by two blank stares. Joseph then recounted everything that
had happened during the night: the angel, the dream and of
his own preordination to raise the young messiah.

After Joseph ended his account, his parents' stares did
not change except for the wrinkle that formed above his
father's eyebrows. There was a long awkward pause and
then Jacob spoke. "I think you have gone completely mad,
had a mental breakdown or something." Joseph let his head
fall seeing that his explanation had failed to convince Jacob
of the truthfulness of his vision. Jacob continued, "This
sounds like the imagination of a desperate man trying to
save his future marriage. How can you be sure this isn't just
your imagination twisting things to make sense of
everything that you went through? I mean, that story is hard
to take seriously."

"All I have is the surety of a peaceful mind and the feeling that only the Spirit of the Lord can deliver," answered Joseph.

"Joseph," Sarah piped up, "I am worried about you son. And like your father, I still have my doubts as to whether or not what you have said is true, because you have been so distraught about Mary. But I will accept it if you do one thing to ease your mother's heart and ensure your vision came from the heavens. When you meet Mary, ask her to recount the experience she had with the angel and if she describes the same experience as the one you saw, then you will know."

"Yes, yes I can do that," answered Joseph.

"If what you say is true, bring us word right away. We will travel to Hebron and make wedding plans there," his mother continued.

Jacob, not being able to believe what was coming out of his wife's mouth, just looked at her with dismay.

"I will do all that you ask," Joseph responded.

Jacob turned around and threw his hands up in the air in complete dismay as to what Sarah was willing to believe. Although he too wanted desperately to believe Joseph, logic was just not allowing him to.

"Father, when you pray tonight, ask God to share with you the truthfulness of my words and then you too will have the peace that I have," Joseph said.

"Go then, and do your mother's bidding," Jacob snapped back.

The sun started to come through the cracks in the door and Joseph realized that the day was beginning and he must get ready to leave.

Just then an excited knock came at the door. Jacob ran to see who could be coming to visit this early in the morning. As he opened the door he saw little six year old Mikilah, the son of his good friend Sadoc. Mikilah was breathing so heavily that he could barely speak.

Jacob kneeled down so he could be at the same level and propped the boy up, for he looked like he was about to collapse. "What is it Mikilah?" Jacob asked.

"The... huh, huh, huh, the Ro..mans came to my house... huh, huh, huh, and told my father that his taxes were past due... huh, huh, huh, and he needed to pay them... huh, huh, huh, immediately, huh, huh, huh." Mikilah paused just long enough to swallow.

"When he asked them for a few days to get the money that they wanted, the soldiers said that wasn't acceptable. They stormed into our house and arrested my mother and father, tied their hands together and took them away to be sold as slaves,"

Mikilah was barely able to finish his answer before tears streamed down his frightened face. Then he added, "I heard the other soldiers say that they are also coming to your house. So I snuck out of my hiding place and out the back. Then came straight here. You must get out of here. If they find me here they will kill me."

Jacob's eyes began to fill with fright. He hugged Mikilah as the boy started to sob heavily to comfort the child and also to hide the fear in his own eyes from the boy. He knew that once the centurion gave the order to confiscate property there was no turning back. He knew it was too late for Sadoc and his family.

Still kneeling and hugging Mikilah, Jacob turned his head to look at Sarah and Joseph, his eyes now filled with spiteful anger. "That treacherous Herod. He told Sadoc and I that we had leniency on our taxes and now he has turned on us."

"That's impossible," Joseph replied. "It's written in your labor contract that in exchange for organizing the import of materials for his palace expansion he would forgive this year's tax debt."

"That paper isn't worth anything now." Jacob was so angry you could see the spit flying from his lips as he spoke. "Herod probably has destroyed all record of any such contract and therefore has turned us into fugitives."

"Do you have the money they are requiring?" asked Joseph.

"No, not here," Jacob's voice was more somber now. His eyes drifted as he tried to think of his options. He knew he only had a few hours before the garrison would arrive at his front door. "I only have five talents of gold here in case of an emergency. I would have to go into town to retrieve the other eight talents and 58 minas," Jacob's voice was quietly fading as his mind was going into deep thought.

Joseph's face suddenly lit up. "Father, I have a plan. Stay here. Do not run. If you run they will track you down and you will appear guiltier than you do now. I will try to be back before they arrive."

Joseph tried to run, but Jacob grabbed his arm and held it fast. "Joseph, what are you going to do?" asked Jacob.

"I am going to go get Amos," Joseph responded.

Joseph darted around the corner of the house and was gone.

Jacob brought the boy to Sarah to see if she could help console him. She took him inside the house but even then you could still hear his sobbing.

Jacob was fighting his instinct to grab his wife and flee. How could Joseph and Amos help them now? After pacing back and forth he resolved on his decision to stay, putting his faith in his son, unaware of what he was planning.

Chapter Eight

The soldiers could be seen a ways off coming up the well-worn path to Jacob's home. Jacob was outside waiting to meet them.

There had been no sign of Joseph. It had been almost two and a half hours since he had left. "Where are you Joseph?" Jacob murmured, his thoughts were becoming tense.

Sarah was still inside, watching the soldiers approach through the front window and trying to keep Mikilah quiet. She was frightened of what was to become of them. She too, was wondering where Joseph was. If he failed in his attempt she hoped that he would not come back and save himself from being dragged away to Rome with them.

As the garrison was getting closer, Jacob could see three people with their hands tied and ankles fettered to each other, stumbling along behind the soldiers. Jacob recognized them as Sadoc, his wife Keriah, and their daughter Cerina.

Sadoc looked tired and he appeared to have been beaten. There was blood on his forehead and his shirt was torn and bloodied, almost falling off his shoulders. Jacob realized that Sadoc must have tried to resist and fought with the soldiers, making matters worse. Now the soldiers would probably take their anger out against Sadoc by attacking his wife and daughter later while forcing him to watch.

Jacob could feel his hands starting to tremble. He was scared, but tried to show no concern over whatever business the soldiers had with him.

The garrison was getting close now. Close enough to smell the horses and hear the marching feet of the men.

Jacob took two steps forward as he saw the centurion give the halt sign and the men all stopped in unison. The centurion took his horse to a gallop to meet Jacob.

"Jacob, son of Matthan, I am Tiberius, centurion of the Galilee Region. I am sent here today to tell you that you are hereby rendered guilty of evading taxes to Rome. I show that 13 Talents of gold and 58 Minas is owed to the Roman Empire. These charges are serious and carry severe consequences if the taxes are not paid immediately," said Tiberius. "Are you able to pay this debt?"

Jacob tried to stall without saying he didn't have enough money. "I am aware of my debt and that it was paid, in part, with my labor to King Herod."

"That is odd, since Herod is the one that alerted us to your unpaid debt, "replied Tiberius.

"I have a labor contract signed by Herod himself absolving me of those taxes. I can get it to show you if you like," Jacob answered back.

"That will not be necessary. Your friend Sadoc had a similar story and we rendered it a lie," Tiberius shot back. "Are you trying to relieve yourself of your obligations as well?"

Jacob straightened himself, his face looking cold and hard, anger starting to take over and rage beginning to take its place. He spoke with a loud voice, his face starting to shake with tension. "I am an honest man and have not done anything outside of the laws that Rome and Herod have strapped me with. I declare that my debt is paid and none other is owed."

Both Tiberius and Jacob were now staring at each other, neither of them budging. Tiberius's horse started to get fidgety, pacing sideways and then being corrected. Tiberius then spoke, "So are you refusing to accept the reality of this charge?"

Meanwhile, inside the house, Sarah, being distracted with what she saw had loosened her hold on Mikilah. He poked his head up to see out the window. His eyes became wide with alarm to see his mother, father and sister tied up. He wrestled out of Sarah's arms. Sarah grabbed for him. But he was already out the front door before Sarah could stop him, yelling, "Mother! Father! What are they doing to you?" He was running at full stride towards his father when his chest met with the side of a soldier's sword, knocking his feet out from under him and he crashed to the ground. Out of his own defensive instinct, Mikilah grabbed a stone as he stood up and looked the soldier in the eyes defiantly.

"Is it true boy? Are those worthless, thieving slugs your family?" sarcastically asked the soldier. The other soldiers started to chuckle.

Sorrow, rage and anger had built up inside of him and he shouted, "My father is a better man than you will ever be." And with that he hurled the rock at the soldier's head. The soldier ducked and the stone missed its target. The soldier brought up his shield concealing his sword, lunged toward the child, moved the shield aside and ran his sword clear through Mikilah's body.

Mikilah's mother screamed a horrible scream – the scream only a mother can give for the loss of her child – a scream of hopelessness and misery. His father tried to free himself of his bonds to run to his dying boy, tears streaming down his face, yelling "NOOOO! NO!" Finally he stumbled and falling to his knees he looked up into the sky howling.

The sword was still in the boy's body when the soldier, pushing with his foot, freed Mikilah from his blade.

47

Tiberius whirled his horse around and galloped at full speed toward the soldier. The soldier didn't have time to get out of the way as Tiberius's foot kicked him with all his might on the side of his helmet. The soldier dropped immediately to the ground unconscious.

Mikilah didn't make a sound, just lay there, looking at his parents, trying to breathe. His eyes showed hurt and shock. Blood started to trickle out of the corner of his mouth as his eyes began to go blank. His breathing becoming less and less labored, slower and slower, until his eyes finally closed and his body went limp.

Mikilah's mother screamed again in agony. She also fell to her knees not understanding the senselessness of it all.

Tiberius was enraged and yelled, "I clearly gave the order this morning not to break ranks without my explicit order." "You two," speaking to the soldiers closest to their downed comrade, "prepare a secured stretcher for him. When we get back to our fort, if he is still alive, he will be flogged and discharged from the imperial army."

Tiberius was livid at what had just happened, but knew that he couldn't show it outside of his anger for the soldier's insubordination.

He walked his horse back toward Jacob. The mother's wailing tugged at his heart. Even though she was a Jew prisoner, he questioned whether he would have the stomach to carry out the lawless sentence that he had given earlier that day of sending them all to Rome.

As his horse worked its way back to Jacob he spoke more to his men. "We are here as honorable soldiers in the imperial Roman army. You are all under my strict command. Anyone who disobeys my orders again will meet the same fate as that young Jew boy on the ground.

"Now, Jacob, son of Matthan. Do you refuse to pay what is owed to Rome?" Tiberius spoke with a tone of anger still in his voice.

Jacob, stared back at the Tiberius, with his own rage in his voice, he replied. "I owe Rome nothing. I owe my life to my God."

Tiberius looked back hard at Jacob. Knowing he could not back down, he declared, "Then by the authority given me by Caesar Augustus, Emperor of Rome I confiscate–"

"HOLD!"A shout interrupted Tiberius. It came from the side of Jacob's home. Joseph appeared from around the corner of the house leading a donkey burdened with two heavy saddle bags. Joseph was leading the donkey slowly but purposefully.

"Who are you?" asked Tiberius.

"I am Joseph, son of Jacob, and have come to pay the tax owed to you by my father and negotiate the release of your prisoners," Joseph answered.

Joseph came to his father's side and then stopped.

"And what do you have in your possession that makes you think you could accomplish such a thing?" replied Tiberius.

"I have 23 talents of gold and 90 minas. Fifteen talents and 58 minas for my father's debt, 7 talents and 20 minas for the debt owed by Sadoc, and 1 talent and 12 minas to split between Rome and Herod for your trouble in coming here," Joseph answered solemnly.

Tiberius liked Joseph's straightforward manner. Joseph was different than other Jews Tiberius had met. He was bold, but there was humility in his eyes and his voice.

"What makes you think I have the authority to accept or reject this offer coming directly from you?"

"Centurion, mighty defender of Rome, you have power to give or take the life of any that you see fit. Even I place myself at risk in bringing this offer. For if you desired, you could take this wealth for yourself, take my life, and still carry out the punishment of my father and mother without anyone questioning your motives," Joseph said. "I sense that you have honor and that you are an honest man wanting to please your Gods. I have made a generous offer that meets, by any measure, the debts of all. Your laws would be satisfied, your men compensated for their work today, and Herod gets a piece of the wealth as he desires. All would be well and we can walk away from this situation." Joseph finished his speech and made a slight bowing gesture to Tiberius.

Tiberius was impressed again with the wisdom and statesmanlike manner in which Joseph spoke. His speech rang true. The offer was generous and would satisfy all involved and it would put an end to an already horrific day. He wanted to take the offer outright and be done with it. However, Tiberius knew backing down now would lead the men to question his leadership.

Out of the blue, Jacob made a sudden movement as if to reach into his side pouch and pull something out. Lucius drew his sword and stepped between Tiberius and Jacob, reacting as though Jacob may have ill intent. Jacob quickly put his hand in the air to show he meant no harm. Then Lucius spoke back to Joseph, "You insignificant Jew, who do you think you are? We could kill all of you and take what we want and still be within our rights. In fact I think we should do just that." He looked back to Tiberius. Lucius' eyes then quickly turned towards Joseph where their eyes met in a cold, but serious stare. Joseph then turned his gaze to Tiberius, as if to say, "I thought you were in charge." Joseph paused for a second then whistled an unusual note. All of a sudden, the surroundings came alive with men standing up from the rocks, trees and shrubbery and on the roof top. Jewish men armed with clubs, bows strung with arrows, and swords surrounded the entire group of soldiers. Amos then came from the back of the house and walked up to stand beside Joseph.

The Roman soldiers all became vigilant, grabbed their swords and readied themselves for battle.

Lucius, fearing an imminent attack, looked at Tiberius and screamed, "Give the order to attack." Tiberius looked around, furious at Lucius for putting him in this situation. This event was quickly escalating, quite possibly to violence. Tiberius swiftly thought through the possible consequences of this battle. Casualties would be high on both sides, even if his soldiers won a victory it would only incite other uprisings and could quickly escalate into a full riot. Then he spoke with a loud voice, "Men, hold your positions!" He held his right arm at a square with his fist clenched, still looking at Joseph, he said, in a calmer manner, "Well played Joseph, son of Jacob. I find myself asking what justice can be done here.

"One of your little ones is dead and without asking for vengeance you have made an offer that satisfies all laws and then some. Only upon finding yourself threatened – though your response was risky and foolish – did you act to defend yourself. I propose this, as a centurion of the imperial army of Rome I accept your offer of payment and release the prisoners. In return, I will give you my captain, Lucius, to do with him what you will in return for the violent death here today and we will part and go our separate ways."

Joseph replied, while Tiberius and Lucius exchanged cold angry stares. "Honorable Centurion, there is no need to require more blood being spilt today. Please take the money and your captain and let's be done with this."

There was complete silence for what seemed an eternity. Lucius and Tiberius still locked stares with each other. Then Tiberius spoke, "Very well then. We have a deal."

Joseph led the donkey to a soldier in the front of the lines, handed him the rope, and said, "It is done."

Tiberius made a motion for his men to release the prisoners. As Tiberius turned to leave, he leaned down to whisper to Lucius, "You owe this lowly Jew your life."

After the soldiers had left, the Jewish militia mingled among each other. Amos and Joseph embraced. Sarah ran out from the house and both she and Jacob hugged their son. Then Jacob said, "Bless you my son, and Amos. You have saved us all." Then Jacob asked, "How was this done?"

Amos answered, "I have been meeting with the Zealot leaders, and having gained their trust I have become their head of financing. Now all funds and donations come to me. Since I had these funds in my possession, I used this access for the money spent today."

As Jacob released another sigh of relief his eyes fell on the path where a small family huddled together holding the lifeless body of their dead son, mourning. He had no idea what to say or how to console them.

Amos, seeing the conflict in Jacob's eyes, placed his right hand on his shoulder and said, "If it is any help to you and the family, the boy did not die in vain. It was this distraction that allowed me and my men to surround the soldiers unnoticed. Without that disturbance we might all be dead by now."

Amos then asked, "Joseph and Jacob, I was hoping, after seeing the efficiency of the Zealot movement firsthand, that you would be more sensitive to our cause and contribute to our coffers?"

Jacob replied, "Amos, I am not one to go against the laws of the land. But I do recognize a debt that requires payment for the money that was spent on my behalf. This I will repay with interest to replenish that which was spent today."

"We have a deal," answered Amos.

Chapter Nine

It was mid-morning and the market place was unusually empty. Most of the inhabitants of Hebron were in Jerusalem for the festival. Mary didn't mind. It was a nice change from the crowded bustling that she was used to in the market place in Nazareth. She was able to casually shop; it seemed to fit her mood. She could even hear her own footsteps on the stone plaza floor. She also didn't miss the dank smell of all the animals. The hillsides were much different than in Nazareth; here the hills were alive with green vines and shrubbery. Many plantations dotted the landscape with olives, pomegranates, figs, quinces, and apricots. Nowhere was there such an abundance of water than in the Jordan valley. There were 25 springs, ten large perennial wells, and several splendid pools.

Mary was excited and nervous to see Elizabeth. Excited because she knew Elizabeth would need her help. She couldn't imagine how hard it was going to be for her cousin going through pregnancy and raising a child in her later years. She felt nervous because she didn't know how to tell Elizabeth all that had happened to her and why she was here?

The thing that would be harder still would be convincing Elizabeth's husband Zachariah of her story. Zachariah was a priest and performed ordinances in the temple in Jerusalem. Temple duties alternated between the other priesthood-holding families. When his family line was chosen to serve, Zachariah would make the 37- mile journey to Jerusalem to perform his duties and then return home.

Mary was getting closer to the end of her trek. It had been a long journey. Normally one would be exhausted after making such a trek, but on the contrary, she felt well and strong and excited to see this journey coming to an end.

Elizabeth loved figs and so Mary bought some while she was in the market and then started her climb up the hills to Elisabeth's house.

....

Elizabeth was struggling with a heavy wash bucket. Water was sloshing over the edges of the bucket as she wrestled it off the edge of the well and then let it thump on the ground. Elizabeth was in her sixth month of pregnancy and was working too hard for someone of her age and condition. After the bucket landed on the ground, Elizabeth grabbed the side of the well as she became light-headed. The surroundings suddenly appeared strange to her and started to spin, everything began to grow light in color, then darker and darker until everything went black. When she awoke she found herself lying on the ground still too weak to stand. She noticed a small amount of blood on her arm from scraping it on the side of the well during her fall. She used her hands to turn her body propping herself up against the well. She rubbed her hand over her belly hoping that her fall had not endangered her baby.

Just as she started to gain some of her strength back she heard some rustling nearby. Elizabeth called out, "Mary, is that you?" "Yes it is I, your cousin Mary," answered a confused Mary.

"Mary, please come around to the other side of the well. I need help to stand," Elizabeth said.

Mary quickly ran over to where Elizabeth was and started to lift her up. She noticed the blood on her arm. "You're injured! What happened and why are you trying to lift this bucket?" asked Mary. "You need to be more careful."

"I am alright, all is well with me," answered Elizabeth. As she stood up she had a bright smile on her face. She placed both hands on Mary's shoulders then nudged her back a bit so she could get a better look at her. Elizabeth said, "Mary, or should I say the mother of my Redeemer?"

Just as these words left her lips Elizabeth let out a yelp. She quickly put both hands on her stomach and said, "My baby even knows whose presence we are standing in. It felt like he just tried to jump out of me a few months early."

"Oh Mary, how blessed are we among women," continued Elizabeth.

"Wait, how did you know I was coming and how did you know I was pregnant?" asked Mary.

"Mary, I don't think I had a normal fainting spell," answered Elizabeth. "When I was on the ground, unconscious, I saw in my mind an angel in white. He introduced himself as Gabriel. He showed me all that has happened to you: his visit to you in your garden in Nazareth; your quick departure from your home. At the end of this miraculous vision he told me to awake, for the mother of my Savior was approaching. That is how I knew it was you,"

Mary let out a sigh of relief and quickly hugged Elizabeth, barely able to reach around her extruding belly, "Thank you! I am so relieved. I didn't know how to explain all of this to you. I didn't think anyone would understand or believe me. I have not told another soul except one friend back in Nazareth before I left. She did not believe me and looked at me as if I was going crazy. I'm afraid this is how most will respond to me and my baby." Then her facial expression fell into gloom.

"Is there something else?" asked Elizabeth.

"It is Joseph. I don't know how to break this news to him. I left Nazareth without telling him. I was afraid he would think I was unfaithful to him," responded Mary.

"Keep your chin up Mary, for the angel also told me that Joseph will arrive in Hebron in five days. Gabriel visited him in a dream as well. He already knows about the baby. He still loves you, wants to marry you and is excited to raise the baby," said Elizabeth. "And don't worry I will be your chaperone while he is here so you can see each other."

Tears of relief started to trickle down Mary's face. All her worry seemed to be melting away.

Mary picked up the bucket of water. Elizabeth put her arm around Mary and they started walking back to the house. "The Lord is not going to let you go through this alone. It is all part of his plan. What do you say we get this water back to Zachariah so he can continue working?" said Elizabeth, comfortingly.

"What do you think Zachariah is going to say?" asked Mary.

"Zachariah is not saying much of anything these days," chuckled Elizabeth in a bright, amusing tone.

Zachariah was busy harvesting some fruit from their orchard while standing on top of a stool. He looked up and saw Elizabeth approaching. He saw someone helping Elizabeth. It appeared that Elizabeth was leaning on this visitor for support. He ran out to be by his wife's side. As he got closer he recognized the looks of this young visitor.

"Dear, this is my cousin Mary. She has come to help me for a time," said Elizabeth.

Zachariah put both hands on his head, and smiled wide. Close to a hundred wrinkles emerged on his face. Zachariah moved his mouth, but no sound came out. Mary wrinkled her forehead not understanding why Zachariah did not have a voice.

He took the bucket from Mary and took her place as Elizabeth's support.

"What is wrong with Zachariah?" asked Mary.

"Let's go sit under the shade of the apricot tree, rest a bit and I will tell you all about it while Zachariah finishes picking the rest of the fruit," answered Elizabeth.

As they got comfortable, Mary asked, "So why can't Zachariah speak?"

Elizabeth said, as she giggled, "You know Zachariah has never been good at following directions, and he is a little sensitive about his age so when he... Zachariah interrupted Elizabeth by waving his arms, grabbed a small tablet and a piece of limestone that was at the bottom of the tree and wrote, looking angry, "I may not be able to speak but I can still hear." He then shoved the tablet to the ground, and turned around to start picking again.

Mary and Elizabeth started laughing. "Oh Zachariah, I was just teasing. It appears you are really sensitive about your age," said Elizabeth.

Zachariah quickly turned his head toward them with an irritated look on his face. This caused Mary and Elizabeth to laugh some more. "You have to admit honey, this is kind of a funny story," Elizabeth said between fits of laughter.

Elizabeth then went on explaining to Mary that when Zachariah was working in the temple the lottery fell on him to have the high honor to minister at the altar of incense prior to the opening of the temple. During this time the angel Gabriel appeared to him and told him that his prayer had been heard and his wife, even in her old age, would conceive and bear a son and that his name would be John. Zachariah then challenged Gabriel and asked how this could be done, "For I am an old man and my wife is well stricken in years." The angel, sensing his doubt said, "Behold, thou shalt be dumb, and not able to speak, until the day that these things shall be performed, because thou believest not my words."

"So Mary, that is why Zachariah has a speech problem. I think he learned his lesson. Second guessing an angel? Not a good idea. That's what he gets for telling Gabriel that I am 'well stricken' in years," Elizabeth giggled some more.

"By the way Zachariah – between you, Mary and I – I'm not the only one that's pregnant," Elizabeth blurted out.

Zachariah quickly turned around throwing himself off balance. The stool shot out from under him and Zachariah, now horizontal to the ground, crashed onto the pile of rotten apricots that he had piled up to be fed to the goats. Mary and Elizabeth could tell he was mouthing angry words but in complete silence.

Elizabeth and Mary laughed some more and then Elizabeth said, "This curse has it perks, not only can't he raise his voice, I win every argument."

…………..

Joseph arrived in Hebron on the fifth day just as Elizabeth was told. He was tired and dusty. He was standing in the market trying to decipher a map that he had paid a man to draw for him giving directions to Zachariah's house.

"This can't be right," Joseph mumbled to himself, stumbling on a stone in front of him, as he turned the map around, and then around again, trying to make heads or tails out of it.

He held it up in front of him trying to see if he could recognize any of the landmarks on the map. Keeping it held in front of him he slowly turned around 180 degrees and then he saw her. The crowd seemed to disappear in front of him because all he could see was her. She was beaming, looking right at him. She had never looked so beautiful. The sun was right behind her giving a glowing appearance to her hair. The map fell out of his hands and on to the ground and he just stared at her. Her smile was radiant. He could tell she was a little anxious by the way her hands were clenching and unclenching in her dress.

Joseph started to walk toward her with every step quicker than the last till he was almost at a run.

Mary stood her ground, grinning from ear to ear waiting for his fast approach. When he reached her they hugged each other tightly and gave each other a friendship kiss on the right cheek. Any more than this would be inappropriate. Elizabeth stepped up to both of them and gave the proverbial throat clearing sound, "huh, huh."

"Joseph, this is my cousin Elizabeth, the one I spoke of in my letter," said Mary.

"Nice to meet you Elizabeth," replied Joseph.

"Nice to meet you as well," answered Elizabeth.

Joseph turned back to Mary, holding both of her hands, he said, "I think I already know the answer to this, but to appease my nervous parents, I need you to tell me what happened to you in your garden."

Mary explained everything that had happened in her garden just as Joseph had been shown in vision by the angel Gabriel. A big grin appeared on Joseph's face and he said, "I knew it. Mary I promise you that I will not leave you from this time on. I will protect you and the child with my life, help you prepare for his birth and will adopt him and raise him as my own."

Relief materialized on Mary's face and then she smiled and hugged Joseph again.

"Well then, you two better get married," exclaimed Elizabeth with a smile.

"I think she might be on to something," replied Joseph. "Let's have the marriage ceremony here in Hebron. I will send a message to my parents and we can have the ceremony within two weeks.

"What about the huppah you made for the ceremony?" asked Mary.

"I will have my Father take it apart and bring it with him," replied Joseph.

"It's time to celebrate," said Elizabeth. "Let's go back to my house. We can all eat a large meal and then for entertainment we can tease Zachariah by carrying on a conversation without any sound and make him think that he has gone deaf too."

Chapter Ten

Tiberius was sitting at his desk in his quarters when Lucius came in.

"You wanted to speak with me?" asked Lucius.

"Yes, Lucius, I am making a change in command. You are being re-assigned to patrol the Jericho valley road. Because it is a more dangerous assignment there will be an increase in pay," said Tiberius.

"What? Why would you do such a thing?" exclaimed Lucius. "We are finally able to serve together again. Don't tell me this has anything to do with what happened at that Jew's home?"

"Lucius, you undermined my authority and stepped over the line," Tiberius shouted back.

"I was protecting you," responded Lucius. "That man could have been going for a weapon."

"You wanted an opportunity to speak your mind and then try to tell me what my next command should be. I couldn't give that command because then it would have appeared that I am not in command. You put the whole garrison in jeopardy. That is unacceptable and I cannot allow it to occur again," replied Tiberius.

Lucius face turned red with anger. He tightened his lips and acted as if he were about to say something else, then stopped and turned his head so as not to look at Tiberius.

Tiberius came from around his desk and placed a hand on Lucius's shoulder. "Lucius, don't you think I have waited for this time when the both of us could be side by side again? But if I let your actions go, I will appear weak and persuaded by friendship. Lucius, as centurion, I am responsible for the safety of all these men and friendship is a luxury that I cannot afford. I am sorry but my decision is final."

Lucius quickly shrugged off Tiberius's hand and said, "You don't have to do this. You are just drunk with power."

"And you have been drunken for the want of it, Lucius," Tiberius shouted back.

Lucius backed out of Tiberius's quarters and said in a cold tone, "You will regret this and our friendship is no longer."

With that, Lucius quickly turned around and walked back toward his quarters. Tiberius, knowing not to take his threat lightly, watched him walk away and then slowly closed his door.

Chapter Eleven

7 months later

It was dark and Amos was cloaked under a dark robe with a hood pulled up to hide his face, traveling up to King Herod's home. He had been summoned to give a report on his progress. Even though it was dark it was still hot outside. Even hotter for Amos with the cloak he was wearing. Amos checked in at the gate and was allowed past. Guards from the house came out to greet him and escorted him inside to a large office brightly lit by candles and oil lamps.

Amos quickly took off his cloak and was relieved to feel the cooler air inside. There were a couple of Roman guards in the office as well. "Guards, please leave us alone for a moment," asked Herod.

The guards saluted, did an about face and dragged the two heavy, large doors to a close that gave entrance into the office.

"This looks like a hard place to work?" asked Amos with a smirk on his face.

"Power and politics, it can have its rewards," responded Herod with a smile. "Please sit." Herod gave a sweeping gesture guiding Amos to a comfortable seat in front of his desk. After Herod had taken his seat behind the desk he looked Amos in the eyes.

"Amos, I won't waste any of our precious time. I will get right to the point. I understand that you have been successful in gaining favor with the leaders of the Zealot movement and are their trusted head of finance," said Herod.

"Yes I have. I believe I am doing well in all that has been asked of me," responded Amos. "In a few short months we should have all the money repaid and secured. You should know that the Zealot leadership is getting more restless and impatient. They want to start implementing their plans,"

Amos then got a concerned look on his face.

Seeing this, Herod asked, "Do you have a question?"

"King Herod, I am concerned about how the money is to be handed over without giving away my connections with you?" asked Amos.

"Leave that up to me, I will let you know when the time comes," said Herod, knowing very well that Amos was to be disposed of when that moment arrived.

Amos answered hesitantly, "Alright, I will wait for your word."

Amos was disappointed that he didn't get a direct answer. He did not feel safe working for Herod and wanted to be done with him as soon as he could. He did not like deceiving his countrymen into giving their money to help defeat Rome, knowing that Herod and Rome were going to be the beneficiaries of it all.

Herod got up from his seat, went over to a cabinet, pulled out a pitcher and poured himself a drink.

"Tell me Amos, does the leadership of the Zealots remain the same?" questioned Herod.

"No Sire. Sadoc, who was next in line for leadership, has become the new leader," answered Amos. "His anger with you and everything Rome stands for has multiplied greatly since his son was killed by a Roman soldier collecting back taxes."

"Yes, I heard about that. How unfortunate for the family," said Herod, absent of any feeling.

Herod was afraid of this. Sadoc was a powerful man and well spoken. He had the ability to incite the whole movement to action, especially now after his son's death. It had been his plan all along to take Sadoc and his family away in order to prevent his coming into power.

"I heard that the soldiers had them in custody when this event occurred. How did they get released?" asked Herod.

Amos did not like where this questioning was headed.

"Well, huh,huh," Amos cleared his throat. "After the centurion had taken Sadoc's family away they went to their next target, Jacob. Being tipped off about the soldiers coming arrival, Jacob's son, Joseph, came to me for help and asked for the funds needed to pay the back taxes."

"And you gave Joseph all the money he asked for?" asked Herod.

"Yes. I had to prove to the Zealots that I could be trusted and finish what they were asking me to do. So I gave Joseph the funds and some of the men and I went with Joseph to help him in case there was any trouble," answered Amos.

"I understand that Joseph used the money you gave him to negotiate the release of Sadoc and his family," continued Herod.

"That is right," responded Amos.

"Did you know what Joseph's intentions were?" Herod continued to question.

"I assumed the money was just to relieve his father's debt," Amos responded sheepishly.

Herod slammed down his cup and shouted, "That would have been a good thing to ask! Don't you think?"

"There was no time to question Joseph in this manner. The soldiers were coming to his home," Amos shouted back.

Herod slumped back into his chair, rubbed his face with his hands, and said, "This Joseph seams to be a real devious fellow."

"Joseph was just doing what he could do to help those in need. He's just that type of person," responded Amos.

Herod answered back, "I fear that these two, Sadoc and Joseph, could foil our plans." Herod remained silent for a moment and then quickly continued, "They are too dangerous to leave alone. They need to be removed.

"Amos, I need to you to do another favor for me and organize a little accident for the two of them – an accident that they will not recover from – if you know what I mean. This needs to be completed within a couple of months to coincide with the time the census will be announced by Rome. Besides, I hear that your friend Joseph is planning on raising a bastard child with his forgiven, but guilty nonetheless, wife Mary," said a sinister Herod, trying to incite a response from Amos.

Amos shifted in his seat nervously, frustration showed on his face as he knew that this was not the time or the place for him to debate this point. Although in his heart he believed it to be true. He believed that Joseph was covering for Mary's pregnancy and that is why he and she had stayed so long in Hebron and had held the wedding there so as to not raise too much suspicion in Nazareth. But these thoughts he was willing to keep to himself.

Amos asked, "Where did you hear this?"

"That is not important, in fact," Herod chuckled. "Reality is not even important. What is important is what people believe, their perception of truth that becomes their reality.

"I have been learning about this messiah that has been prophesied to come into power, to sweep his enemies under his feet and to become a new king to rule forever. Isn't this why the Zealots are arming themselves, to prepare for this mighty warrior and king? Do you believe in this messiah as well?" Herod finished.

Amos did not reply or move in his seat.

"I didn't think you would want to respond to that, Amos. Let me quote to you a passage from the great prophet Isaiah. '"For unto us a child is born, unto us a son is given: and the government shall be upon his shoulder.'" '"The government shall be upon his shoulder,'" Herod repeated the last phrase again slowly to add emphasis.

"Look around you Amos. The Roman Empire has never been stronger. Their might and strength is greater than anyone can fathom. Do you really think that someone could be born, rise up with a bunch of misfit, angered Zealot militia and conquer all of this? Think about it Amos. If a messiah or new king is to be born and conquer Rome I don't think now would be the time to try. I believe the suspected timing of this new king is misguided and is not as close as the believers think," continued Herod.

Amos was surprised at the knowledge that Herod showed regarding scripture and prophecy. He knew a response was needed. "Egypt was at its highest strength when Moses brought the children of Israel across the divided Red Sea." Amos replied, proud to have been so quick on his feet.

"Yes, yes, that is true," Herod agreed. "But Moses had also warned the great pharaoh," Herod was purposefully sounding sarcastic. "Let's see if I can remember, yes, seven times to 'let my people go.'" Herod began to laugh out loud.

"I tell you what Amos. If all of a sudden the Jordan River is turned to blood I will willingly give up my throne and never look back. But until then," Herod said with a clenched jaw, "I am your king and I rule this land. I will not allow anyone or anything to disturb that – especially not this nonsense of a conquering hero messiah".

Amos pursed his lips together, and answered angrily. "Helping you with the Zealots was supposed to be the last task required of me to be free of our agreement. Additionally, did you know that Joseph has been a close friend of mine since childhood?"

"Amos, Amos, Amos, I am afraid I am going to have to modify our agreement so you will do whatever I want you to do. Besides, because of your friendship with Joseph it should be easy to get him to trust you. I think you can figure out the rest. Remember it is for the safety of your own family," answered Herod. "So you will do as you are told or you will feel how a true king rules with the government upon his shoulder. Do you understand where I am coming from?"

Amos's face showed dismay at what was being asked of him. He realized that he was being taken advantage of and that Herod was never going to let him out of this arrangement. He realized that what Herod said regarding the coming of the messiah made sense. The prophecy did sound foolish when put in this context and not knowing what else to do Amos responded, almost in a shout, "Fine! For my family, I will do as you ask." With that Amos lowered his head, put his cloak back on and headed back towards his home.

Chapter Twelve

Joseph was coming in from his workshop for dinner after a long day of deliveries. He came in the door, dropped his bags, shuffled over to his chair and fell into it. He was exhausted. Mary was out back bringing in laundry. She was seven months into her pregnancy now and her belly was showing prominently.

"There you are Joseph, I was wondering when you were going to come....Oh what is that smell?" Mary, interrupted herself. She stood several feet away from Joseph plugging her nose.

"What?"Joseph asked.

"Dear, before I can come any closer, you need to take a bath. Where were your deliveries today?" Mary said, still plugging her nose.

"I don't think you're smelling just me. I delivered a whole furniture set to the home of Crendon," replied Joseph.

"Crendon the cattle farmer? Was the furniture delivered in the cow stalls?" asked Mary, her voice sounding nasally.

"No, but after I delivered the furniture set, Crandon wanted to show me what he was doing to help migrate the cattle better and I think I stepped in a pile of fresh cow muck," answered Joseph with a light chuckle trying to brush away the tension.

"And you still have your shoes on. Joseph, how many times do I have to tell you to keep your shoes outside," Mary responded. Joseph began to stand up. "Ah Ah Ah, take your shoes off first," Mary said sternly.

Joseph sheepishly took off his shoes and took them outside. Then, to make Mary feel better, came over and started to rub her back.

"Is this making it better?" Joseph asked.

"You're on the right track," Mary chuckled.

Mary's sense of smell had amplified by about ten times since she had become pregnant. Even little smells seemed to set her off. Joseph tried to be sensitive to this, but he was always amazed at how sensitive her nose was. Luckily she was over the sickness stage of the pregnancy. Once Joseph brought a fresh beef roast home to prepare for dinner, as payment from a customer, and placed it in the kitchen by

Mary. To him there was no odor, just a little blood. She took one look, put her hand over her mouth, ran outside and threw up her lunch.

Joseph and Mary had been back in Nazareth for four months now. They had stayed in Hebron for three months until Elizabeth delivered her son John.

Their wedding had been fantastic. That night, prior to the ceremony, the whole town of Hebron got involved when Joseph was making his march through town, the reception line must have stretched 1,000 ells (approx. ½ mile). Everyone held their lanterns up high and made celebratory gestures to Joseph.

It was tradition to celebrate the bride and groom as queen and king. Mary was even placed on a throne as the guests arrived, while Joseph marched in surrounded by guests who were singing praises and toasting him.

Then Joseph, followed by his guests, proceeded to where Mary was seated and placed a veil over her face to symbolize his commitment to clothe and protect her and also to keep physical attractiveness in proper perspective to her soul and character. This was the first time either saw the other that day.

The actual ceremony took place outside under the huppah that Joseph had made. Joseph didn't remember many of the words that were said that night, he was just happy to finally be married.

Most people in Nazareth had forgotten the earlier rumors and assumed that the baby growing in Mary was Joseph's. Joseph and Mary did not make the truth known to anybody for fear of how they would react to them and the baby when it was born.

Joseph finished rubbing Mary's back and had just sat back down in his chair when there was a knock at the door.

Joseph opened the door to see an anxious Amos standing in the doorway. "Joseph, did you know that your shoes sitting right by your door really stink?" Amos said.

"So I have been told," responded Joseph.

Joseph opened the door wider, made a sweeping gesture and said, "Amos, come in and rest. I can show you the baby's nursery, we almost have everything ready for him."

"No Joseph. Actually I was wondering if I could talk to you alone for a while," said Amos, acting nervous and looking behind him as if to see if anyone was watching.

"Sure. You can come with me as I try to clean off my shoes. Walk with me around back to the well as I get some water," responded Joseph.

"I would like that," answered Amos, glad to leave the public view in front of Joseph's house.

As they walked to the well, Joseph asked, "What is it Amos?"

"We have been friends since childhood and we have always confided in each other and told one another the truth no matter what the circumstances were, haven't we Joseph?" asked Amos.

Joseph replied, "Is this about Mary and I and the baby? I know you have not been totally convinced of what I have told you regarding the angel. I have felt your resistance to this. But I have also appreciated your not speaking your mind publicly."

Amos was looking disturbed, seeing that it was going to be more difficult than he had thought to reveal everything about Herod, his deception and this horrible obligation that he was under. "Joseph, what would you think of me if I told you I had to do something that went against everything I believed in?" asked Amos.

Joseph stopped walking, turned to Amos and then said, "I would ask why and then convince you of why you shouldn't do it," replied a concerned Joseph. "What is it Amos? You know you can confide in me with anything."

Amos, losing his confidence, just could not bring himself to let Joseph in on his terrible secret. He then said, with a sudden change in his demeanor, "Joseph, how is it that you are so perceptive? I was going to tell my father what I felt about you and Mary, but you are a good friend and even though I may not believe you in all of this I will keep it to myself," replied Amos.

"Thank you Amos, you are a good friend and no matter what you think of me you are always welcome in my house anytime," Joseph said.

"You're welcome, Joseph," Amos answered with a guilty tone in his voice. "I need to go run another errand. I will see you around Joseph. Thanks again for this talk."

Joseph sensing something else was wrong and seeing Amos's sudden need to rush off as a bit strange, almost inquired from Amos further. But he decided to let him go and he got back to the task of washing his shoes.

Chapter Thirteen

Sadoc was just finishing up supper when he was alerted that Amos was at the door to visit with him. Being the new leader of the Zealot movement, Sadoc had plain clothed guards with him at all times to protect him from any danger. They also checked all visitors to ensure that no one entered unannounced. If anyone tried to sneak past the guards they would be met with deadly force.

"Please, send him in," ordered Sadoc. Sadoc was waiting to hear from Amos as to the status of their finances to see if they had enough resources at their disposal to fund their plans.

"Amos, glad to see you, come sit down with me and have a cup of wine," said a generous Sadoc.

"No thank you," answered Amos. "I need to talk with you in private. I was hoping we could retire to the coolness of your balcony."

"Why certainly." Sadoc replied. Sadoc's balcony looked over a ravine and faced west so the sunset could be seen and give light in the early evening hours. It provided a wonderful view and the architecture that went into its construction was not a small feat. The balcony spanned 40 feet across without any support beams underneath and stood at least 30 feet off the ground. Sadoc was always happy to show off elements of his large estate to guests.

As the two were walking up the stairs to the balcony, Sadoc asked quietly, almost in a whisper, "What is the status of our funds? Do we have enough to act?"

Amos answered back in the same quiet tone, "Yes. This is why I wanted to speak with you. We need to discuss how to keep the funds safe while implementing your plans." Amos knew the funds were not ready, but wanted Sadoc to be comfortable and distracted.

"Wonderful, this is great news, Amos. Great work," Sadoc replied.

They both sat down in chairs admiring the view, when Sadoc said, "I have a plan for you. If you break our wealth into small portions and disperse them into separate accounts under names that only you have access to it will keep anyone from taking the whole of it if we are compromised. We have more recruits coming in daily to support us and many have been secretly storing weapons for us to use when the time comes."

"Sounds like you have it all figured out, Sadoc," said Amos. "I believe we have a viable plan."

With this Amos got up from his chair and walked over to the rail on the balcony. He was about to lean up against it when Sadoc called out quickly as he walked to his side, "Amos, don't lean on that rail, it is too weak! I need to have it replaced," warned Sadoc. Sadoc was now standing next to Amos, both of them staring at the weakened rail.

"Thank you for telling me Sadoc. That would be a nasty fall," replied Amos.

Amos, now seeing an opportunity, slowly stepped backwards to get good footing then quickly grabbed Sadoc under his arms, and shoved him with all his might into the rail. The rail made a loud cracking sound and almost gave way, but still held. Sadoc quickly turned around in bewilderment to see Amos coming for him again. Before he could yell out Amos grabbed Sadoc by the throat and started to choke him.

Sadoc's feeble arms were not strong enough to overcome Amos's hold and terror quickly appeared on his face. Sadoc stared into Amos's face which now looked fiendish and evil as he continued to keep a tight grip on his throat. Amos could feel Sadoc's strength fading. Knowing that if the guards found him on the balcony, they would know of his murderous deed, he made another attempt to push Sadoc into the already weakened rail and this time the rail gave way completely and Sadoc went over the edge. But before he fell completely he grabbed a fistful of Amos's clothes around his chest and held fast.

This pulled Amos down face first on the balcony, dangerously hanging over the edge as Sadoc continued to keep his life or death grip on Amos. Sadoc looked up into the eyes of Amos and said, "Why are you doing this? What about my family?" pleaded a frightened Sadoc.

"I'm so sorry, I didn't have a choice. I had to do this," replied a tearful Amos.

Sadoc's hand was shaking and losing its grip. He looked down at the ground and knew that he would not survive the fall. He then looked back at Amos and said, "Amos, you have lost your soul." His hand slipped. Amos watched as Sadoc's body silently fell. Sadoc never lost eye contact with Amos until his body hit the ground with a low-sounding thud. Amos could tell that Sadoc was dead.

He then started screaming out, "Guards, guards! Sadoc has fallen! Come quick." Two guards were already coming up the stairs due to the earlier commotion. They came up to the edge of the balcony where Amos was still lying.

"What has happened here?" asked one of the guards.

Amos responded with tears still on his face. "I leaned on the rail and it gave way. Sadoc tried to save me and in doing so he pulled me back, but that caused him to go over the edge. I tried to hold onto him but it was no use and he fell."

The guard blew on a bull's horn sounding an alarm. Three other guards and Sadoc's wife and daughter came out of the house and ran up the balcony stairs. Sadoc's wife was running towards the edge when one of the guards stopped her and told her that she shouldn't look right now. She wrestled out of his grasp and ran to the edge. "SADOC!" she yelled, looking down to where his body lay. Sorrow and agony were etched on her face as she started to wail but no sound escaped her mouth. She collapsed on the balcony in a convulsion of sobs.

Amos, seeing the pain that he had caused, needed to get away. He left the balcony and the estate. His guilt was almost overwhelming. He was feeling the pains of a damned soul.

. . . .

News of Sadoc's death spread like wildfire through Nazareth. The members of the Zealot movement were in disarray. They were confused and argued amongst themselves as to what should be done next and who should be the new leader. After weeks of deliberation, campaigning, and meetings, Amos was chosen to be the new leader of the Zealot membership. Amos did not campaign or even aspire to this position, but was rather shoved into it by other members because of his work in expanding donations.

This news made it up all the way to Herod. He found it amusing that the one who was proving to be the demise of this movement was now their leader. "Now, Amos, kill Joseph and the plan will be complete," Herod thought to himself, while sitting at his desk sipping wine from his cup.

Instead of being excited with this new honor, Amos was depressed, knowing that his election had only been made possible because he had killed the past leader in cold blood. His demeanor had changed. Amos was no longer the happy-go-lucky person he had once been, always looking on the bright side and having fun. His past actions had put him in a downward spiral of depression and guilt. It made him sick to think of what he had done, leaving Sadoc's once happy wife to become a widow with only a daughter as an heir. And then the knowledge that he still had more to do to keep his family from the dangerous reach of King Herod made him contemplate hurting himself on a number of occasions. There seemed to be no way out of his situation.

He finally made up his mind. The only thing that made any sense to him, the only thing he felt would allow him to keep his family intact and relieve him of this agony for his actions: he determined to kill Joseph and then himself.

Chapter Fourteen

Gaius rode into Nazareth looking urgent and rushed to deliver a message from Rome.

Gaius had been hailed earlier that day and ordered to retrieve and deliver Rome's message to all citizens of the Galilee region. This was not going to be a small task. As head communications courier, he was able to assign representatives to go to the outer reaches of the region to help him distribute the message in a timely manner.

Gaius ran to the wood bulletin sign in the middle of the town square, took out a nail and hammer, and fastened the letter from Rome with its official seal of the eagle to the sign. He then turned around and shouted the message aloud to the inhabitants.

"Citizens of Nazareth, subjects of Rome, it is decreed by the powerful emperor Caesar Augustus that all men, women and children of the Roman empire must be counted and taxed. All males and heads of household must return to the city of their birth within one month's time and there report themselves and their family to complete this census. All citizens not accounted for, if found not to have complied with this decree, will be punished with excessive financial penalties. Those penalties, if not paid, will result in confiscation of all property and those heads of household along with their families will become property of Rome."

Gaius finished reading and did not look to see the reaction of the townsfolk or try to answer any questions. He got back on his horse and bolted out of town as fast as he had come.

The mumblings of the people gathered in the town square became louder and louder as they started to sense the consequences of what had just happened. Plans, business, industry and other travel would need to cease just to appease Rome with their census so they could count how many subjects they had in their ever-growing empire.

Joseph and Mary were at his father's home when the news reached them.

"Joseph," Mary said, "What are we to do? The baby is due within weeks. Everything we have ready for the baby is here in Nazareth."

"I'm not sure Mary," Joseph replied. "I guess we will need to take things both for us and the baby."

"Are you sure?" Mary asked. "What about the cradle, the trunk, the wash basin for laundering diapers and the extra baby clothes?"

"We'll take it all Mary," Joseph assured her. He then went over a mental checklist of what needed to be done to accomplish such a thing. "Our wagon needs to be fixed, the axel needs to be reinforced and the walls need to be replaced. I think I have the supplies left over to complete all that," Joseph thought to himself.

"Mary, when we get home, will you start getting supplies and provisions ready? I want to leave soon. We don't want you going into labor on the trip," Joseph gave Mary a smile and a wink.

"I will come with you and help you," Sarah said.

"Travel safe son, and take care of Mary and…" Jacob hesitated a bit.

"Go ahead and say it," Joseph replied. "I know what you're thinking."

"Take care of Mary and our future grandson," Jacob finished.

Jacob and Joseph shared an embrace and then Joseph, Mary and Sarah left for Joseph's home.

……..

Amos approached Joseph's home in a disheartened and agitated state. He fought the war inside his mind between what he had determined to do and just ending his own life.

Amos carried a long, skinny package wrapped in sackcloth. As he walked to the side of Joseph's home he found Joseph's body lying on the ground – his head hidden underneath the wagon. The wagon's wheels were off and the axel was supported by a wood block.

Joseph heard footsteps and slid out from underneath the wagon just enough to see who had come.

"Amos, good to see you friend," Joseph said happily. He then slid back underneath the wagon. "Can you believe the arrogance of those Romans in calling for this census? Now that we have prepared everything for the baby to be born here in our home, I am not looking forward to this trip to Bethlehem. I am worried for Mary and what effect the travel will have on her. What brings you here friend?"

"Joseph," Amos said sounding serious, "I can no longer be called your friend, for what I have come to do is worse than an enemy's act and not worthy of any friendship."

"Amos quick joking around and hand me that short javelin tool. I need to force this brace into place," Joseph responded without even looking up.

Amos saw the pointed tool and handed it to Joseph, thinking in his mind that this would be the last time the two would touch.

Joseph started to struggle prying on the axel brace. Amos backed away from Joseph and started unwrapping the package he had brought with him. It was a sword from the Zealot weapon stockpile. It was long and heavy. It didn't look shiny or ornate, but it was strong and would do fine for what it was intended to do.

As Amos brought the sword out from the sackcloth, his hands became sweaty, and his legs were shaky. Amos took two steps toward Joseph, raised the sword about waist level, his face showing intensity as he gripped the sword. He stopped all of a sudden. His face slackened and he put the sword down. He looked at the block of wood supporting the wagon. It was sturdy enough but given a quick kick it could easily become dislodged. Joseph was holding the sharpened tool straight up and down just above his chest. If the axel of the wagon came down now the tool would pierce Joseph's heart and it would appear to be a terrible accident.

Amos, sidestepped over to the far side of the axel, lifted up his foot.

Just then Mary came around the corner and said, "Joseph, where did you put the... Amos I didn't know you were here. Did you come to see us off?"

Surprisingly, Amos fell to his knees, covered his face and started sobbing. Joseph crawled out from under the wagon, got to one knee, and asked, "What is the matter Amos? What has been going on with you these last few weeks?"

"Joseph," Amos responded between sobs, "I am a murderer."

"What are you talking about?" inquired a concerned Joseph.

"I murdered Sadoc. I am the one who pushed him over the edge of his balcony, and I had come tonight to kill you with this sword, Joseph," said Amos.

"What!" Mary yelled.

Joseph started to back away from Amos and Mary came running up to his side.

"What are you saying? Tell me this isn't true. Why? Were you promised money?" questioned Joseph.

"Herod threatened to kill my family if I didn't help him stop the Zealots by collecting the money and then surrendering it to him. But when Sadoc became the new leader Herod threatened me again unless I killed him," cried Amos.

"What does this have to do with me?" Joseph questioned further.

"Herod was mad that I helped you negotiate Sadoc's release. He did not want a Jew thwarting any part of his plan – especially not one who could negotiate so successfully. Herod is a mad man and will stop at nothing to make sure that no one challenges his power," said Amos, tears staining his face.

"Joseph, I resolved to kill you with this sword and then kill myself, to save my family," said Amos.

"What about me and my family Amos?" Joseph yelled.

"Joseph, I can't hurt you or Mary. I don't care what happens to me anymore. I will no longer do Herod's bidding," Amos continued. "Joseph, you and Mary are not safe here in Nazareth. Herod will send others. You and Mary must leave now."

"Mary," Joseph was still looking at Amos in disbelief after what he had just heard. "Grab just enough provisions for a couple of days and do it quickly."

"But Joseph what about the baby's things in the nursery?" Mary responded.

Joseph walked backwards, keeping his eye on Amos. He then walked quickly over to Mary, held her face in his hands, and stroked her hair out of her face and spoke softly but firmly. "I promised God that I would protect you and the baby with my life if necessary. And if we stay here any longer that may be exactly what I'll have to do. Do not worry about the baby's things I will figure something out. But Mary, we leave now."

Amos walked over to Joseph and started to speak but Joseph quickly picked up the sword, held it out in front of him. "Amos, stay away from me and Mary. Do not come any closer," Joseph ordered. Joseph couldn't believe what his life-long friend had turned into, anguish showed on his face.

Joseph stood between Mary and Amos with the sword held ready for action. His grip was tight and his knuckles white, his muscles were flexed and focused, ready to swing if necessary. Mary darted inside to get what they needed.

"Mary, what is going on out there?" asked Sarah. Mary was visibly shaking.

"I don't know. Amos, has just confessed to killing Sadoc and told Joseph that he was sent to kill him as well," Mary said. "Joseph said to grab just enough provisions for a few days and that we are going to leave now."

"Oh my!" Sarah cried with concern. "Here. I have already prepared food for the journey. I will put it in the bags if you want to run to get extra clothing for you and Joseph."

Mary started to run to the bedroom and then stopped and turned back and Sarah said. "When will you be coming back?"

"I don't know when or if we are coming back," Mary said rapidly.

Sarah thought for a minute and then went to her own knapsack and pulled out some swaddling clothes. "Here, I was going to finish preparing these and then give them to you after the baby was born, but take them now," Sarah answered.

"Thank you Sarah," Mary answered back. "Now stay inside until Amos is gone. I don't want him to know you are in here."

Mary quickly gathered everything. It only took a few minutes and gave Sarah a hug. Then Sarah said, "Take care of yourself and the baby. Jacob and I will bring all the rest of your belongings with us." Mary hugged Sarah again and then ran back outside to rejoin Joseph, while Sarah watched with concern from the window.

Amos realized that this would be the last time that he would ever see Joseph again. He thought for a moment and said, "Joseph, take my donkey. It will help with your escape. It is the least I can do. You'll find it around the front of your house. I am so, so sorry Joseph. I don't know what else to say."

"I don't want you to say anything. I do not want you to see or speak with me again," Joseph retorted. There were a few seconds of silence and then Joseph continued, "Once Herod discovers that you alerted me to his plan he will kill you. You know that, right?" Joseph said the words tensely yet with some compassion.

"Not if I kill him first," Amos replied, having a sinister look in his eyes.

Joseph was again shocked at the change that had come over Amos. Evil had completely taken the place of his once pleasant nature. Only vengeance remained.

Mary went and got the donkey, set the saddle bags on its back with their scarce belongings and handed Joseph the rope. Joseph finished wrapping the sword back up in sackcloth.

Joseph picked up Mary and placed her on the donkey's back and left – all the while keeping an eye on Amos.

Now all alone outside, Amos repeated his last statement to Joseph in a hateful whisper, "Not if I kill him first."

Chapter Fifteen

Rage burned in Amos's eyes like the wrath of a fiery furnace. He could see nothing but revenge on Herod. It was Herod that had brought this evil upon him and had taken away his innocence and it would be Herod that would pay the price with his life.

....

Later that night Amos made his way to the gate of Herod's home. He waited till after dark. He approached the guards wearing the same black cloak he had on his last visit and presented invitation papers to the guards.

Amos had used the previous meeting papers he had received to forge the ones he presented this night.

The guard looking over the papers wrinkled his nose a bit, looked over the top of the papers to see Amos and said, "Funny, Herod told us before dark that he had completed all his business and that he was not to be disturbed."

"Well, someone forgot to remind him that I was summoned here by his own pen," Amos said thinking quickly on his feet. The guards looked at each other with suspicion.

"Look, why would I come all this way unless the king called for me to be in attendance?" Amos said to their implied suspicion.

"I am not going all the way home unless I get word from Herod that he does not want to see me. Besides, I have vital information about the Zealots that he needs to hear tonight regarding impending plans. I don't think you want to be the ones blamed for denying Herod this information, do you?" Amos continued, trying to use fear to gain access.

One of the guards spoke up and said to the other, "You stay hear and watch our guest. I will inquire if indeed his presence is requested."

"Wait," Amos spoke up, "that won't be necessary." He walked closer to the guards. He gave a motion for them to come closer as if he were going to tell them something in secret. The guards – not suspecting anything sinister – leaned in close to Amos.

Amos had his arms crossed in his cloak concealing sharp daggers in each hand. When the guards leaned in, Amos made a quick motion bringing his crossed arms up. In one smooth motion Amos had the blades on the outside of the neck of each guard and then by uncrossing his arms slit the throats of the guards before they could make a noise.

Both guards fell to the ground, blood was pouring out of their wounds. Death for each of them was certain.

Amos knew that he did not have much time. Other guards would find the two bodies soon and sound an alarm. He ran through the gate and into the vast front garden looking onto an outside patio. Amos could see Herod being

91

fed grapes by a female servant while another danced in front of him.

"Perfect," Amos thought. "This distraction is all I need." Amos, hidden behind a bush, threw off his cloak which hid his bow and arrow. He knew he only had one shot. He was determined to make it count. He quickly assembled his bow and nocked his arrow. He pulled back on the string and took close aim. He then whispered to himself, "The government shall not be on your shoulders any longer."

Just before shooting off the arrow, Amos felt a sharp stabbing sensation in his back. He looked down and saw a sword blade protruding out of his stomach. The string of his bow lost its tension and the arrow fell to the ground. Amos turned his head to see another guard with a grim look on his face as he pulled the blade out.

Amos could feel life draining from him. He coughed and he could feel blood spattering from his throat. He fell down on the ground as the knowledge of his past evil doings came flooding to his mind. An agonizing fear raced through his mind. He started to feel sleepy, and then everything went dark. Amos was gone.

. . . .

The guard brought Amos's body to the patio and placed it before Herod. "What is this?" Herod demanded

"Amos, your confidante with the Zealots broke through your gate by killing the guards," the guard responded. "I found him in your front garden with an arrow trained at your heart. I acted fast and killed him before he killed you."

Herod stood there dumbfounded for a minute trying to make sense of this. Then the answer quickly came to his mind and his eyes went wide.

He realized that his whole plan was unraveling. The money collected for the Zealots was dispersed in various accounts with Amos being the only one who knew where all the accounts were and under what name they were deposited. Getting the money now would not be possible.

Sadoc was dead and now Amos was killed trying to assassinate him. This could only mean one thing. Amos had told Joseph everything and Joseph was still alive.

Herod looked at the guard and gave a quick order. "Take two men, and go to Joseph's home. If you do not find him there send out an alert to our Jericho highway patrol to be on the look out and if found, to kill him on sight."

"Yes sir," The guard pounded his fist to his chest in a customary salute, turned around and was off.

Chapter Sixteen

Joseph and Mary slipped out of Nazareth unnoticed. Luckily they were able to join a caravan that had just started toward Jerusalem.

Meanwhile, Herod's guards reported to Herod that Joseph was gone and that it appeared that he had left in a hurry. Herod did not know what Amos had told Joseph. But if he had told him of Herod's plan to thwart the Zealots and Joseph was able to reach any member of the leadership of the movement, his plan would be ruined and a full scale riot would be on his hands.

Word was immediately sent by couriers:

> *To all patrols of the Jericho highway, search all caravans traveling toward Jerusalem and be on the lookout for Joseph, son of Jacob. He will be traveling with his pregnant wife, Mary. If found, kill him on sight and bring back his body as proof.*

. . . .

Lucius was sitting by his fire resting with his patrol. He was thinking about what his life was like back at the fort doing the job of an officer and captain. He didn't belong here training new recruits to patrol a highway and transporting criminals. "This is all Tiberius's fault," Lucius thought to himself. He rehearsed the last conversation he and Tiberius had had again and again. "He was jealous of my authority and wanted the leadership all to himself."

His anger wasn't as heated as it had been the day he'd left, and he had regretted saying what he had said at their parting. Even though on the surface he claimed to blame Tiberius, he really blamed Joseph for all of this. He couldn't fathom how Joseph, a common Jew, managed to scheme against him – making him out to be a fool and turn Tiberius against him.

Lucius's moment of self pity was interrupted when the soldier on post came to him and said, "We have a rider approaching."

"Can you tell who it is?" asked Lucius.

"No, but I can tell that he is Roman and by the speed of his horse I would imagine he is a courier," said the soldier.

"Maybe this courier brings my transfer back to the fort," Lucius thought to himself.

Lucius went over to where the courier would come into their camp and waited for his arrival.

Gaius came riding up to the camp at full speed and didn't slow down until the last second. His horse quickly came to a stop. Its body was heaving up and down with its heavy breathing. Gaius dismounted and went to meet Lucius. He had been riding most of the night – ever since he got the message from Herod. His horse was used to being ridden like this and had been trained to run at high speeds for several hours. The sun would start to rise in about an hour or so. Lucius's men were on the night patrol and were about to lie down and rest.

"Hail Lucius," Gaius said.

Gaius, what brings you out at this time of night?" Lucius replied.

"I have an urgent message from Herod," Gaius said as he held out a parchment.

Lucius opened the message and motioned a soldier to bring a torch to give him light so he could read the message. As he was reading, a little smile came across his face. "Well that jackal has finally made someone mad enough to want him dead," Lucius began thinking to himself again. "If I bring back Joseph's body maybe I could negotiate my return to the Galilee region as centurion, with Tiberius being transferred out."

Lucius finished reading the message then gave it back to Gaius. "I assume you have other patrols to deliver this to before morning breaks," said Lucius.

"Yes, I believe I will be riding throughout the morning and into the afternoon," Gaius replied. With that Gaius finished giving his horse water, mounted his saddle and was off.

"Men, put out the fires and mount up. We have a fugitive to catch," shouted Lucius.

There was silence and everyone stared at Lucius.

"I said MOVE!" Lucius shouted again.

This time his men jumped to their feet and scurried around, getting ready to ride.

Lucius barked his instructions. "Our fugitive's name is Joseph, son of Jacob. He is traveling with his pregnant wife. They just left Jerusalem yesterday. They couldn't have gotten far even if they joined a caravan already on the move. We will ride north in five minutes."

. . . .

"Joseph, I can't ride or walk any further. I am too fatigued and in pain. We have been riding all night. Please let us rest some more," Mary pleaded.

"Mary, we have already fallen behind the caravan enough that I can hardly see their torches. The sun is starting to rise. It is not safe for us to rest this far away from them. We have to catch up before they leave for today's journey. We must keep going," Joseph replied.

"I can't," answered Mary. "My body cannot move any further. I have to stop."

Joseph, having pity on Mary, lifted her off the donkey, looked around and carried her up a hill under an overhang obscured by some brush. He gently set her down and used his outer robe as a pillow to put under her head so she could lay down in a little more comfort. As soon as her head touched Joseph's robe Mary fell asleep.

Joseph looked down at her. He knew this journey was hard for anyone, let alone someone almost 9 months pregnant. He had been pushing her as hard as he dared without endangering her health. But now he feared he had pushed too hard.

He looked down toward the caravan and could see movement in their camp. He knew that it wouldn't be much longer before they would start to pack up and be gone, leaving him and Mary too far behind to ever catch up.

Joseph went back to the donkey and opened up the saddle bags and took inventory of their food and water. They had just enough to last the journey with one extra day's rations in case something went wrong. "Thank you, Mother, for preparing extra," Joseph said out loud to himself.

Joseph knew that another caravan would probably be coming through just after nightfall. He decided to feed, water and hide the donkey close by and then watch over Mary as she slept. Joseph himself was weak from lack of rest, but he knew if he didn't stay hidden and vigilant there would be trouble.

Before Joseph put the donkey behind the rocks near the overhang where Mary was sleeping, Joseph pulled out the sword still wrapped in the sackcloth. He unwrapped it and remembered holding it up to Amos and felt sadness as he thought of their friendship coming to such a quick and dramatic end. He shook his head back and forth to force these thoughts from his mind so he could focus on what he needed to do.

He took the sword, which felt heavy in his exhausted hands, and staggered up the hill to sit by Mary and watch over her. Before he sat down he looked down the road and could see the caravan starting to move out. "This is it," he thought. "I need to keep us safe until the next caravan comes." He then sat down and leaned on the sword.

. . . .

The sword slipped from Joseph's grip and he was jolted awake. It was starting to get dark. He was trying to get a fix on his bearings. "Why is it getting dark?" he thought. "No, it couldn't be," he said in a whisper.

He quickly looked and saw that Mary was still asleep. They must have slept all day.

Joseph ran out of their hiding spot and looked down the road in both directions. As far as he could see there wasn't any caravan in sight. "Did we miss the next caravan?" Joseph thought to himself in fear. Joseph couldn't believe that he had slept for so long. He went over to Mary and gently woke her up and explained that they had both slept all day and that he feared that they had missed the next caravan.

"Mary, I think that we are going to have to start traveling. We can't take the chance that we missed the caravan," Joseph explained.

There were only two things that could have happened. One, they had missed the last caravan so they needed to catch up. And if they traveled through the night they just might do that. Two, they were leaving prior to the next caravan's arrival and it would, more than likely, catch up to them.

The sun was large on the horizon and made their shadows long behind them. There would be a full moon this night, which would be good and bad. Good that they would have some light to guide them and bad because it would make it easier for others to spot them on their journey.

Mary and Joseph were only on the road for minutes before the sun peeked below the horizon. They were still weary from their previous night's travel.

Mary and Joseph did not speak a word, keeping as quiet as they could, so as not to draw attention to themselves.

After a couple hours of travel, Joseph could see some lights up ahead. Could that be the caravan? Something looked different. It appeared that the lights were moving towards them.

Joseph stopped the donkey and looked at Mary. She was looking at the lights coming closer as well. "What do you think it is?" asked Mary.

Joseph stood silent for a second and then he saw clearly what it was. It was Roman soldiers on horseback and they were coming fast. Joseph quickly looked around to see where they could hide but realized it was too late. The soldiers had already spotted them and would be upon them in seconds.

Joseph grabbed the sword from his side bag and said, "Mary, get down from the donkey and stay behind me."

The horses came in at full speed and almost slid to a stop about 20 feet from Joseph and Mary. Lucius was in front and recognized Joseph right away. Joseph recognized him as well. He couldn't forget that day at his Father's house and what had occurred.

Lucius dismounted while the other soldiers trained their arrows at Joseph. Joseph stood little chance against soldiers armed with bows and arrows. Add to that his lack of training with a sword, he knew he, his wife, and the baby were in dire circumstances.

"Joseph, Joseph, Joseph," Lucius said slowly. "I was hoping we would meet again. I wanted a chance to thank you in person for ruining my career. What makes matters worse is that the person that ruined my career is a despicable Jew.

"But I believe in silver linings and one has presented itself here tonight" Lucius continued. "You see Herod sent a message saying when we found you to kill you on sight."

"Why does Herod have any business with me?" Joseph asked.

"I don't care," replied Lucius. He started to walk closer to Joseph.

Joseph held the sword out in front of him and said, "Stay back, don't come any closer."

"Or what, Joseph, are you going to kill me?" Lucius said with a chuckle. "I tell you what Joseph. I will make a wager with you. I agree that my men will put down their bows and will not get involved while you and I fight to the death and the prize is that pretty girl behind you."

"I don't want to fight you Lucius," Joseph said.

"You don't have a choice," Lucius shouted back as he was taking off his gloves and removed his sword from its sheath.

Joseph tilted his head toward Mary and whispered, "Get on the donkey and hold on tight." Mary did so immediately and Joseph gave the donkey a quick slap on its hind end and the donkey ran off into the dark.

"Joseph, don't you think we are able to track her down?" Lucius said sarcastically.

Joseph responded sounding confident. "I just didn't want her to see me kill a man."

This angered Lucius and he started to walk to the left of Joseph. Joseph followed Lucius's movements with the tip of his own sword.

Joseph then spoke with a stern assurance, "Lucius, I promised my God to protect my wife and her holy child with my life."

"Well my friend, that is exactly what I plan on you doing," Lucius responded, sounding cocky.

"Then do your worst, Lucius, for my God and I will do ours," Joseph shouted back.

With that, Lucius lunged forward and tried to strike Joseph. Joseph barely was able to move the sword fast enough to block Lucius's strike. The blow was so hard that it nearly knocked Joseph to the ground. Lucius's men erupted in cheers for their leader.

Lucius, knowing that his opponent was no match for his strength, skill and combat experience, started to play with Joseph a little by walking clear around Joseph like a leopard would its prey.

Joseph feared for his life. The strength of Lucius's first blow had caught him off -guard. He was unsure how he would get out of this alive.

Lucius quickly made another strike. This time Joseph moved to block but only partially hit the blade away from him and Joseph had to quickly dodge out of the way or Lucius's sword would have hit him.

Joseph barely regained his balance, and stood up straight, just to have Lucius hit him in the stomach with the hilt of his sword. Joseph doubled over in pain. Lucius met

Joseph's downward movement with the hilt of his sword, hitting Joseph under his chin, sending Joseph reeling headlong backwards onto the ground.

Lucius's men were cheering louder and started making wagers of their own.

Joseph scrambled to get up and hold his sword up once more. His chin felt like it had exploded and he could feel the blood trickling from a wound. Joseph moved quickly away from Lucius as he was trying to regain his composure.

"This may be easier than I thought," declared Lucius. "When I bring back your dead body to Herod I may get my position back that you ripped from me."

Joseph tried then to go on the offensive and rushed Lucius swinging his sword. Lucius dodged the strike and punched Joseph on the side of his face, sending him down to the ground a second time. This time Joseph's sword flew out of his hands, away from him, toward the other soldiers.

Joseph started scrambling to get his sword back. Lucius quickly jumped on Joseph's back, turned him over and put his knee on Joseph's throat. Joseph grabbed Lucius's knee with both hands as he began to choke. Lucius brought his sword straight up readying it to plunge through Joseph. Joseph closed his eyes and heard Mary scream out "JOSEPH!" Then suddenly a bright light appeared. Like a crack of thunder a voice shouted, "STOP!"

When Lucius looked into the light he saw a man in white holding what appeared to be a flaming sword. Lucius quickly got off of Joseph and started to cower away in fright. Lucius's men tried to control their frightened horses and nearly fell off.

Joseph rolled away from Lucius, holding his throat and coughing. He recognized the personage in the air as Gabriel.

Then Gabriel spoke with a voice booming from the heavens. "Lucius, why do you try to kill the earthly father to the Son of the Almighty God? The baby the woman is carrying is a holy child. God covenanted with Joseph that if he was vigilant in protecting the baby and its mother, they would be kept safe. And now I have been sent from Almighty God to keep that promise. If you pursue your quest to hurt Joseph or his wife, even if it is a thought in your mind to bring them harm, I will strike you down and place the wounds of death in your body. And in that instant, you will be taken back to Him that created you.

Now Gabriel was standing between Joseph and Lucius and his men. In that instant eyes were opened to see a heavenly army behind Joseph with swords, horses and chariots covering the road, hills and the entire valley.

Fear struck Lucius and his men so greatly that they all scattered, riding their horses every which way trying to escape, until the night was again quiet. These men were never heard from again.

Gabriel let down his sword, looked at Joseph, and then spoke. "Joseph, you have proven yourself worthy and will not be molested any longer on your journey. But you must move quickly to Bethlehem for the time of the baby's birth is coming soon."

Joseph stood up, bloody and bruised, and said, "Thank you for saving us."

"Thank your God who sent me and your thanks would be thanks indeed," replied Gabriel.

Mary ran to Joseph's side, with tears still running down her cheeks. "Joseph, I thought you were going to be killed."

After hugging her husband, she faced Gabriel and gave a courteous bow. Gabriel smiled and said, "Glory to God in the highest and on earth peace, goodwill towards men."

With that, he and the other heavenly hosts were gone and Joseph and Mary were left alone in the darkness once again.

Chapter Seventeen

A few days had passed since the incident with Lucius. After spending a few days in Jerusalem to observe the Sabbath, they had continued on.

Joseph and Mary had traveled alone since the night Lucius and his men had found them without seeing any other caravan or group. They didn't mind the privacy since the fear of any harm coming to them was gone completely now that they knew a heavenly army was at their back. This allowed them to rest for as long and as often as Mary needed.

Joseph's wounds were healing well. Mary stitched up Joseph's chin with a strong hair from the donkey's tail and the bruise on his cheek was starting to fade some.

They were just getting their first glimpse of Bethlehem. Nightfall would be coming in a few hours. Joseph wanted to get settled in town before the sun set. This would be possible if they didn't take any more rest stops. At this point Mary rode entirely on the donkey since her feet had swollen to the point that her shoes had rubbed blisters on her heels and sides of her feet. Plus the fatigue in her back and legs was becoming great.

As they began to get closer Mary started to feel more and more agitated and could not seem to get comfortable at all. Then it began.

"Joseph," Mary exclaimed, "My water has broken from my womb. The baby is coming."

"What?" Joseph could see the sheer panic on Mary's face. He then looked to see how lmuch of the journey they had left. They would need to hurry if they were to get to Bethlehem in time for the birth. Joseph did not want to try to deliver the baby without being able to send for a midwife quickly if needed.

Joseph started to pull the donkey faster. "I will get you to a restful place as fast as I can," said a concerned Joseph.

The first real contraction had hit her and she grimaced in pain. Joseph thought to try the *Khan* (inn) just outside the city. They would be able to reach that within a few minutes.

A khan was a one level structure used to give rest to weary travelers after a day's journey and would allow these travelers to tend to their animals and tie them up safely for the night. There were sometimes places to bathe. It also included stalls or niches to accommodate merchants, servants and their supplies. There was always water for animal and human consumption and small shops where one could replenish supplies to further their journey. Most every place inside a khan was very public. Privacy was not the main goal. When a large festival or events were to take place in a city the khans would be overflowing with people, animals and merchants.

The donkey, for the most part, was cooperating nicely and was moving quickly. Upon reaching the opening to the khan, Joseph said, "Mary, try to stay calm. I will see if we can find room here for you."

Joseph ran into the courtyard. The stench of animals and their waste was almost overpowering. He had never seen so many people stuffed into a khan before. Joseph started asking anyone if they could direct him to the manager of the khan. Finally, Joseph located the manager and said, "Sir, my wife is in labor. Do you have any room where she might deliver her child? We have money and are able to pay."

"What do you think?" retorted the manager. "There are wall to wall people and animals in here. Every niche and cranny is filled. I can barely keep enough water in the troughs for the animals. Listen, even if there was room, there is no place for privacy for your wife to deliver in here. I am certain your wife would not want this."

The manager started to walk away and Joseph cornered him once more. "Sir, please, if not here, do you know of another place close by?"

The manager's face looked angry and frustrated at being kept from his duties on a very busy night. He then looked into Joseph's eyes and saw the sincere concern and urgency. His anger melted, then his eyebrows lifted slightly, and he said, "I may know of such a place. It would be much more private than here. Walk with me and I will show you."

They both walked outside. The manager gave the torch he was carrying to Joseph and pointed up a small hill where there was an open cave near the top.

"That is where I keep my personal animals – to keep them separate from all the vagabonds that go through the khan. There is fresh straw and a place to build a fire. You will be safe in there," the manager directed.

"Thank you, kind sir. How much do I owe you?" Joseph said gratefully.

"You don't owe me a thing," the manager replied and quickly went back to work.

Joseph quickly led the donkey to the cave and after making a soft straw bed carried Mary inside and laid her down. Mary had beads of sweat on her forehead and face. She was still grimacing in pain with each contraction, but she remained calm and tranquil.

There she delivered the Savior of the world, the Prince of Peace – sent to this earth with love from a Heavenly Father so all may have a chance to return.

Joseph held him in his arms. "He is finally here," he said to himself. For the first time in a long time Joseph felt like he could finally rest. They had done it. Together they had been successful in bringing forth the longest anticipated and possibly the most protected birth of all time. He began to think of what this young life held in store for the world. The young Lord opened his eyes and looked at Joseph. Joseph had never seen such a tender and precious face, so calm and peaceful. "Hello Jesus," Joseph said with a smile. Then he gently handed him to the welcoming arms of his mother.

Mary held him in her arms and Joseph helped her wrap him in swaddling clothes and lay him in a manger of straw. Then, after feeding the Christ Child, Mary and the Christ Child rested.

. . . .

During that very night shepherds who tended the sheep used for temple sacrifices were on a hill near Bethlehem. The shepherds were getting ready to bed down for the night.

"Now Shem, let me show you how to gather the sheep for the night," said Mathon, head shepherd of the flocks. "You need to make sure all the sheep are here so they will not become a meal for other animals."

Mathon brought his 11 year old son, Shem, to help with the other shepherds in tending to the flocks. Shem was so excited to be out with the men for the entire night. It made him feel important, especially since he was usually stuck at home with his three older sisters while his father helped with the sheep.

From the hill they could see all the activity going on in Bethlehem. They had never seen it so busy.

"I am so glad not to be caught up in that crowd," said Simon, another shepherd.

"You got that right," said Mathon.

"Well we better get some sleep. With all those people down there I'm sure there will be a big need for sheep at the temple. We will need to get an early start," continued Mathon as he started to bring out his sleeping roll.

"Shem, you better get your things over here to sleep by me," Mathon looked around but couldn't find Shem. "Shem, where are you?" hollered Mathon.

"Over here father," Shem called back on the other side of the rocks. Mathon walked over and saw his son sitting down looking at the hustle and bustle of Bethlehem.

"I wonder what's going on down there?" asked Shem.

Mathon sat down by his son and saw the wonder in his eyes, then said, "There are people from all over Judea down there. They must have all kinds of stories of their adventures."

Shem's eyes became wider and said, "Can we go down there?"

Mathon ruffled up Shem's hair and said, "No Shem, now is the time for sleep. Now come with me and get your things ready. We will have an early start tomorrow."

"Fine, but tomorrow can we walk through the market? I can't wait to hear some of their stories," replied Shem.

"Sure we can," said Mathon.

Mathon helped his son get everything ready and arranged for sleep, kissed him on the forehead and said goodnight. But instead of Shem's customary response of 'goodnight father' Shem's eyes were focused on the stars behind them in the sky. It looked like they were dancing.

"Father, look!"

Mathon turned around and saw what had astounded Shem. There was a bright star that had appeared in the sky – one that he had never seen before. It was brighter than all the other stars in the sky. And it seemed that the smaller stars were dancing around it. No wait, the stars were coming closer to them.

Then right in front of them a brilliant light appeared and an angel from the Lord stood in its midst.

"Shem, get behind me," shouted Mathon.

The other shepherds stood up and were backing away, shading their eyes from the light.

Then the angel spoke calmly, "Fear not: for, behold, I bring you good tidings of great joy, which shall be to all people. For unto you is born this day in the city of David a Savior, which is Christ the Lord. And this shall be a sign unto you; Ye shall find the babe wrapped in swaddling clothes, lying in a manger."

While all the shepherds were marveling at this messenger there appeared in the sky a host of angels praising God and saying, "Glory to God in the highest, and on earth peace, good will toward men."

Then as fast as they had come they were gone, except for the bright star. Mathon, looked at Shem, and said, "Well Shem, I think you will get your wish of getting off this hill after all."

"Where should we go to see this newborn?" asked one of the shepherds.

"I think we should follow that star," replied Mathon.

....

A few hours after the birth of Jesus, still in the throws of night, Joseph saw men approaching the bottom of the hill leading to their cave. "Surely they wouldn't be coming up here. No one knows we are here except for the manager of the Khan. Who are these men?" Joseph's thoughts were racing through his mind.

He jumped to his feet, grabbed his sword, and spoke confidently, "Who goes there?"

"Peace be unto you, we mean you no harm. We are merely shepherds that have had an astonishing message brought to us this night from heavenly beings singing praises to our master and king. They are the ones who told us of a wonderful birth and that we should come and find a child wrapped in swaddling clothes and there behold our salvation," spoke Mathon, the lead shepherd.

112

"Then welcome, come look upon the Savior of the world," Joseph said.

The shepherds marveled at the sleeping Jesus. Mary awoke and saw the curious visitors with Joseph standing by. Another shepherd stood up and said, "This night will be celebrated until the end of time. For this night redemption has come into the world."

After a few more minutes the shepherds gathered their things and prepared to leave. Mathon said to Shem, "I think we will be the ones telling stories in the market place. Everyone needs to hear what has happened tonight. "

They went straightway into the city to tell all of the marvelous events that had befallen them.

Mary turned to Joseph and said, "I desire that we not broadcast the birth of Jesus so that he does not turn into a spectacle. He is a small baby and does not need to be disturbed by strangers."

"As you wish Mary," Joseph replied.

Chapter Eighteen

18 months later

Joseph walked out of his workshop. It was still early in the morning. The air was brisk, but the sun was shining. Joseph started to walk towards the house and saw Mary playing with Jesus. They were both on the ground playing with sticks drawing figures in the dirt. Jesus started laughing and then Mary started to tickle his waist, grabbed him and rolled over so he was sitting on her stomach. Now they were both laughing. Joseph was happy just to watch this moment unfold.

Joseph and Mary and Jesus were adapting well to Bethlehem. Joseph was establishing his carpentry business again and had a list of customers.

Jesus had started walking when he was about 12 months old and now he was saying his first few phrases. Talk around town had died down some since the shepherds had broadcast what they had seen to the whole region it seemed.

His thoughts began to drift back to that night in the cave and the days after Jesus' birth. He remembered when they took Jesus to the temple to declare his name. This is where it was made official that Joseph had adopted Jesus as his own son. While they were there a man came up to them eagerly.

"Hello, my name is Simeon and I have been waiting to see the promised Messiah for a long time. It has been revealed to me by the Holy Ghost that I should not see death until I have seen the Lord's Christ. Today the spirit has guided me to the temple and has also revealed to me that the baby you hold in your arms is indeed the same Christ child," Simeon declared.

"May I hold him?" Simeon asked.

Without saying a word, Mary handed Jesus to Simeon. After marveling at Jesus, Simeon praised God and said, looking into the sky, "Lord, now lettest thou thy servant depart in peace, according to thy word: For mine eyes have seen thy salvation, which thou hast prepared before the face of all the people; A light to lighten the Gentiles and the glory of thy people Israel."

After he handed Jesus back to Mary and thanked them for giving him this opportunity, Joseph said to Mary, "Do you know him?"

"I have never seen him before," answered Mary.

"Could he have heard the news from the shepherds?" Joseph questioned.

"Even if he did, how did he know we would be here at the temple or recognize us? There are other parents with their children here today as well." Mary said with curiosity.

"We are not going to be able to keep the news of Jesus to ourselves any longer. There will be others that will seek him," Joseph said.

"Like Herod?" Mary said with some irritation.

Joseph was coming out of his daydream and heard Mary call out for him.

"Joseph!" Mary happily hollered. "Come join us, we are having fun."

As he was walking toward Mary and Jesus he began to wonder... even though it had been 18 months, was Herod still seeking for him? Shaking that thought from his mind Joseph ran over to where Jesus was standing.

"Come here, you," Joseph said to Jesus with a smile as he play-tackled him and rolled on the ground while Jesus erupted in laughter.

Like every son, Jesus had a wonderful bond with Mary. She was the one to pick him up when he fell or scraped his knee, which had been quite often since he learned to walk. She seemed to have a way of wiping away his tears and making him happy again. It was very seldom that the two of them weren't smiling and laughing together.

Jesus had a different bond with Joseph. It seemed to be playful in nature as well, but it was also more subdued and reverent. Every time Joseph came into their house Jesus would run to him with open arms and yell, "Papa!" Joseph would sweep him up in his arms and twirl around. Then later he would just sit in his lap as Joseph told him stories. Jesus wanted to be by Joseph when he wasn't working and often wrapped his tiny hands around Joseph's finger and followed him around.

……..

Unknown to Joseph and Mary, men had been seeking them –, but not for Joseph – this time they sought for Jesus. They came from the east and were not familiar with Judea. They decided that it would be good for them, since they were not citizens of the region, to let Herod know of their business.

Herod had just come away from his morning meal with some of the chief priests and scribes of the Pharisees. Herod was met by his servant Seron.

"Sir, there are men to see you from outside of Judea and say they wish to ask the location of the New King of the Jews," said Seron with a wrinkle in his brow.

"What?" Herod replied. "They must be mistaken. Are you sure they did not ask for the location of me, the current king of the Jews?" Herod responded.

"You heard me correctly. I had them repeat their question twice," answered Seron.

"Give me a minute to freshen up and then send them into my chambers," Herod ordered.

"Yes Sir," Seron responded.

Even though he did not put much weight in prophecies, Herod was aware of the prophecy of the birth of one that would become king. Herod asked in his mind, "Is it possible that there are those that believe the prophecy has come true? Even if it is merely perceived that the prophecy has come true, this may cause revolts and in the least battles with the zealots – small as they are now."

Herod was sitting in a large chair when the men entered.

The men were obviously wealthy men since they were wearing brightly colored and costly apparel; it was also obvious that the men were foreign for their style of dress and demeanor was different than those of Judea.

"Hail, King Herod," the first man said. "My name is Baron, and these are my companions Herek and Jashal."

"Peace be unto you as you travel in our country," Herod answered back.

"What brings you to Judea?" Herod questioned, not wasting any time in getting to their business.

"We have been awaiting a sign given in the heavens that a baby had been born," answered Herek. "The sign was given months ago as a new star shone in the sky. We have followed this star into your country and need to inquire if you know what city we need to go so we can see the one that is born to be 'King of the Jews',"

"And for your trouble we would like to give you these pieces of gold as a gift," Jashal said. He produced a velvet bag that jingled as he laid it on a table in front of him.

"That is very generous of you," Herod said.

Herod then sounded a small bell and Seron entered.

"Yes Sir?" Seron inquired.

"Have the chief priests and scribes left yet?" Herod asked.

"No Sir, they are getting everything in order for their departure," answered Seron.

"Go ask them to come in here. I am in need of their knowledge. Ask them to bring in their scrolls as well." Herod said.

"Right away Sir," responded Seron.

After a lengthy discussion, it was decided that Bethlehem, the city of David, was the city prophesied to be the birth place of the new king.

As Baron, Herek and Jashal were preparing to leave, Herod asked in a polite, sincere voice, "Once you find the child, bring me word so that I too may be able to go and worship him."

"As you wish King Herod," answered Baron.

. . . .

Later that evening, Baron, Herek and Jashal came into Bethlehem and went to the home directly under the star and came to Joseph's home.

Joseph saw the visitors and went out to see if he could help them.

"We are foreigners to your country come to worship the child prophesied to be king of the Jews," Baron said.

Joseph, with a bewildered look said surprisingly, The child you search for is named Jesus and is inside with his mother."

"May we see him?" asked Baron.

"Yes, I will go get him," responded Joseph hesitantly.

Baron, Herek and Jashal all got down from their camels and started to unload items from their bags.

Mary, being a little bashful, slowly brought Jesus out to meet their guests. When they saw Jesus they all kneeled and bowed their heads and said, "Lord and Master we come to worship your birth."

Jesus remained calm and simply stared at the men. Baron was the first to stand and present something to the child.

"I give unto you gold from Persia as a gift to a new king," said Baron.

"And I give the gift of frankincense from the coast of Oman," said Jashal.

"And I too have a gift to give; I give the new king the sweet scent and uses of myrrh from Arabia," Herek added.

These gifts were significant. In the Old Testament, the Queen of Sheba visited King Solomon and brought him gold and spices. Gold and frankincense are rare, valuable and precious commodities. These items represent the best to be offered from different parts of the world. Since these visitors recognized Jesus as a king, it makes sense that they would give these most precious and rare items. These gifts were reserved for only the highest of honors.

Frankincense is a sweet-smelling sap which hardens and then was used for incense or for perfume. Frankincense was burned as incense in the temple because of its rare, wonderful smell.

Myrrh is also a sweet-smelling sap from a tree. But its uses are quite different from those of frankincense. The most practical uses Joseph and Mary would have had for it would have been its medical uses as an ointment.

"Thank you for your generosity and kindness," Joseph said as their visitors continued their worship of Jesus. "These gifts will be used to aid in the young child's upbringing."

Jesus was calm and respectful throughout this experience. He sat up straight and tall and acted as if he knew the manner in which such gifts were given.

Both Joseph and Mary were impressed with Jesus' behavior. They both looked at each other and marveled.

"You're most welcome. I would like to give my thanks for the opportunity to be in your house and worship this young king," said Jashal.

"I add my thanks–"

"–And mine as well," Baron and Herek said together.

"If we might stay a while longer we would like to celebrate this occasion with a feast," Baron said. "We have plenty to share and have brought some of the finest chefs in our land to prepare the meal."

Joseph agreed almost immediately but then saw a perturbed glance from Mary and she mouthed the words, "What about the dinner I was preparing?"

Joseph simply shrugged his shoulders and mouthed back, "We can eat that too?"

Then Mary gave a polite smile to her guests and Baron clapped his hands together and said, "Wonderful, it is settled. We will send for our procession outside the city at once."

The feast went well; everyone seemed to be enjoying themselves. The food was magnificent. The spices and method of cooking were a sight to behold.

Jesus continued to be treated as royalty by the entire procession. Each time anyone passed Jesus they gave an admirable bow.

Baron came up to Joseph and put his arm around him and said, "Joseph, how wonderful it is to be alive in this time. Joseph, we are aware of your heritage of royalty from David – one of your great past Kings. You must be proud."

"Proud indeed," Joseph answered. Joseph was unsure how much these men knew about the prophecy and decided not to tell them about Mary's virgin birth or that he was not Jesus' biological father but the one chosen as a father figure to raise Jesus.

"Baron, I have a question. How is it that you came to know where to find Jesus?" Joseph inquired.

"We stopped and inquired of Herod to know what city Jesus was to be born in and the scribes sent us to Bethlehem," Baron responded. "He is interested in worshiping the young king as well and wanted us to bring him word when we had found him."

Joseph could not believe what he was hearing. A prickly sensation shot down Joseph's spine as he realized the impact of such information if it were to get back to Herod.

Joseph turned to look Baron in square in the eye and said soberly, "Baron, I implore you not to return to Herod. He is not one to be trusted and I fear for the safety of my family if he is told where we are."

"We understand your fear," responded Baron with the same sober tone of voice. "Last night we had a dream in which an angel told us not to return to Herod. We will go back to our country another way. Your location will not be revealed by us, but be aware, he does know we came to Bethlehem,"

Joseph's mind was racing. "Just because he knows what city we're in doesn't mean he knows how to find us. There are a lot of children in Bethlehem that are around the same age as Jesus," Joseph thought to himself.

This line of thinking calmed Joseph's fears a little and he walked back with Baron to enjoy the rest of the celebration.

Chapter Nineteen

"It has been a week since those men from the East left here," Herod yelled as he slammed down his fist on his desk.

"Well Sir," Seron said, trying to explain. "It may have taken them awhile to find the child and then they tarried there for a time,".

"No," Herod yelled. His fists clenched so tight that the whiteness of his knuckles showed. His face was as red as fire, his jaw tightened and his eyes were filled with rage. Beads of sweat were starting to form on his forehead as he put his hands under the edge of his desk and heaved it over on its side with a huge crash, sending its contents scattering about the room.

Guards came storming into the room thinking there had been an accident. To their astonishment all they saw was Herod in a raging tirade. They had never seen him this out of control.

"They made a fool out of me," he screamed. "No one makes a mockery of me! Who do they think they are?" he continued in the same loud tone.

"I will not allow anyone to think that there is a chance for any to rule BESIDES ME! I am their King and no one is going to change that. They think that they may raise up someone to challenge me. I will smash their hopes to dust.

"This day I will be known as Herod the Great and show that no one can defeat me," he continued, yelling as loud as anyone had ever heard him yell. "This day I give a decree and sentence every baby boy, two years and younger in Bethlehem to death. KILL THEM ALL! Maybe that will end this FOOLISHNESS," He ended and stomped out of his office.

The guards stood there unsure of what they had just heard or what they had just been ordered to do. Did they hear him right? They were to kill every baby boy in Bethlehem younger than 2 years old?

This seemed to go beyond Herod's other ruthless acts like the time when he had had his brother-in-law drowned because he felt that his growing popularity threatened him. His two sons had met the same fate – ordered killed because of his endless paranoia. And when he feared that his wife Miriam was having an affair he had had her murdered in a jealous rage.

Herod was also known for doing other terrible things to individuals who crossed his path or got in the way of his plans.

But this was a new low. Such a mass murderer was unheard of. Was he serious or just delusional with madness?

This question was answered when Herod came storming back into his office with a parchment written fast and sloppy, but readable. He signed it and gave it his official seal. Then he gave it to his servant and said, "Give this to Gaius and send it to Tiberius."

"This is to be carried out tomorrow night!" screamed Herod, handing the parchment to Seron.

"As you desire Sir," Seron said, as he hesitated to take the parchment out of Herod's hands. Herod seeing his reluctance shoved it into his hands, violently turned Seron around and shoved him towards the door.

Seron barely kept his balance but managed to keep some composure. Herod then walked over to a table that displayed rare foreign vases and with one arm swept them off the table and watched them crash on the floor.

He then looked at the guards and said, "Clean this place up before I return." He then stormed out of his office.

. . . .

Gaius came riding fast into the fort yelling for Tiberius. Tiberius, hearing the commotion, came rushing out from his quarters to see Gaius jumping off his horse and running toward him with a parchment in hand.

"Urgent orders from Herod. This is to be carried out tomorrow night," Gaius said, breathing heavy.

Tiberius opened the parchment in haste and was surprised by the manner of the writing. But after he started to read what was ordered his heart sunk, his shoulders slumped and his knees felt weak.

"What?.... Why?....How can this be?" Tiberius thought to himself.

"Gaius, what am I to do with this?" Tiberius questioned.

Gaius, standing at attention, looking straight forward, said, "Sir, I have delivered your orders. What you do with them is up to you," Gauis spoke the last of his words with a compassionate look at Tiberius.

Tiberius put the parchment back in Gaius's hand and said trying to sound convinced, "Thank you. Tell Herod we received his orders and will proceed."

Gaius gave a customary salute and bow, then mounted his horse and was off.

Tiberius didn't have a choice. He had made a vow to Rome and dereliction of duty could bring a sentence of death to the insubordinate.

As senior centurion it was his duty to address the entire cohort and give them their orders.

A cohort consisted of 6 centuries and each centuria contained 80 men; therefore, to fill a full cohort, 480 men would be involved.

The next day the cohort gathered to hear their assignment. Tiberius was dressed in full uniform. He knew that he had do deliver these orders without wavering, otherwise his leadership would come under question.

"Men, we have direct orders from Herod. Every boy in Bethlehem two years of age or younger must be put to death. This mission needs to be in haste and completed in one night. Men, tonight is that night. We will ride into the city after midnight. You have the right to enter any house in Bethlehem and search any area that is needed. Once you find a child you will end his life quickly and move on. If parents of the children can be subdued then so be it, but if they become violent or threaten you then they must lose their lives as well. That is all," Tiberius ended and then left the men to themselves as he went back to his quarters.

Tiberius walked back into his quarters trying to think of what he had just done. Frustrated, he yelled and shoved all the maps and papers on his desk to the floor. He was tired of carrying out ruthless orders to satisfy a madman's paranoia or passion. Those who wrote such orders never had to witness the aftermath of their orders or hear the screams of the victims as they cried to know why they were being punished.

It didn't take long for Tiberius to decide that these orders would be his last and he started to prepare his resignation papers to be given to his superior, Pontius Pilate.

. . . .

It was dark. Mary and Joseph had put Jesus to bed and were preparing to retire themselves.

As Joseph looked over the sleeping Jesus he asked Mary, "I wonder what his life has in store for him. What will be required of him to be the salvation of this world?"

"I don't know Joseph, time will tell. But he is the Son of God and as such is destined to be great," Mary responded. Mary then looked confused.

"What is it Mary?" Joseph asked.

"Joseph, something doesn't feel right tonight," Mary said. "I have a bad feeling," she continued.

"I'm sure you will feel differently in the morning. You know how overprotective you can be at times." Joseph responded.

"Maybe you're right, sleep well darling," Mary said as she lay down next to Joseph.

Joseph fell right to sleep and started to dream. In his dream he was on a mountain top. A mountain that he had never seen before. The angel Gabriel was there and asked Joseph, "What do you desire Joseph?"

"I desire to know the importance of the life of Jesus." Joseph replied.

"Then let it be as you desire," Gabriel said. "Look." He motioned with his hand toward where he wanted Joseph to look.

Joseph looked and beheld the Savior reaching adulthood -- being of good stature and being obedient to all the commandments in every way. Knowing his true identity as the Son of God, Joseph saw Jesus baptized by his cousin John and then the Holy Ghost landing on him as a dove and the voice of God saying, 'This is my beloved Son, in whom I am well pleased.'

He saw him fast for forty days and nights, being tempted of the devil and not succumbing to his temptations. He saw him performing mighty miracles -- miracles that only those with the power of deity could do. He turned water into wine. He healed those that were sick and caused those that were blind to see. He saw Jesus even raising those who had died. He saw him cast out devils that tormented people. He saw him calm the waves of the sea by simply speaking, 'Peace, be still.' He saw Jesus walk on water and bid one of those who followed him to join him on the water and so he did. He saw him feed 4,000 with only seven loves of bread and a few small fish. He saw throngs of people following him as a lamb follows a shepherd.

He saw him throw out the money changers in the temple who were defiling God's house. He saw him confound the wise and educated by speaking plainly regarding the prophecies of old. He explained that it was he, Jesus, who had come to save mankind. And there were many other things that he saw Jesus accomplish. He saw that he was kind and merciful to all that he met and he only had love for all. Joseph couldn't have been more proud.

The vision came to a close and Gabriel asked Joseph, "What else do you desire?"

"I desire to see how salvation is to come to the world," Joseph responded.

"Then look," Gabriel said and he gestured as before.

Joseph looked, but this vision was different. The previous one had been marvelous to see – this one seemed dark and disheartening.

Joseph saw Jesus walking up a hill late at night being very sorrowful and heavy. He saw him fall down alone on his knees and plead to his Father above, 'O my Father, if it be possible, let this cup pass from me: nevertheless not as I will, but as thou wilt.' Later he continued to pray, 'O my Father, if this cup may not pass away from me, except I drink it, thy will be done.' He saw an angel appear to help strengthen him. Then Jesus became distraught and appeared to be in agony and pain. He was being tormented both body and spirit. His whole body began to tremble and his sweat turned to blood.

Gabriel then said, "Behold the Savior of the world is paying the price and feeling the pains of all men that he might win their souls and because their worth is great, the cost is exceedingly great. This pain is so great that it will cause Jesus, the greatest of all, to tremble and bleed from every pore so that all may not have to suffer if they repent and follow him. If this were not so, all mankind would be lost. This can be likened to a man facing a candle that may burn the flesh of his arm, Jesus must face that flame which is likened to the sun, to make his sacrifice an infinite and eternal atonement – one that satisfies every last bit of the law. With this he shows his love and devotion to mankind, the world and the heavens. He deserves our praise and glory forever."

Joseph, crying at the sight of this heart-wrenching scene wanted to run up and hold Jesus and tell him that he was there and that everything would be alright. He could not bear to see any more of the suffering of Jesus and said between sobs, "Please don't make me watch any more, I can't bare it."

Gabriel, kind but stern, said, "Look."

After Jesus had suffered such agony and pain, Joseph saw men coming toward him. He was then betrayed and taken away to be tried by false accusers. He saw those that hated him blindfold him, slap his face and mock him saying, 'if you are the son of God tell us which one of us slapped you.' 'You are not the son of God; you are the son of a carpenter.'

Joseph, hearing this yelled, "You fools, why can't you see? Why won't you believe? Joseph's crying became bitter seeing that Jesus was suffering in some part because it was Joseph who raised him.

Joseph then saw a mob screaming, 'Crucify him, crucify him,' and so Jesus was released to the mob. They had him beaten and flogged with whips having sharp bits of bone at the end to tear the flesh and cause the most pain. Then a crown of thorns was pressed into his head, cutting him deeply all the while those around him mocked him, hit him, and spat on him saying sarcasticly, 'Hail, king of the Jews.' A beam from his cross was then strapped on his back but finding him to weak to carry it another was forced to carry it for him to the top of the hill Calvary. There they drove nails into his hands, feet and wrists and lifted him up on a cross. His body was shaking terribly. His face looked dejected and in anguish.

In the midst of this pain and rejection, Jesus showed such love and mercy. He looked up into the heavens and said, "Father, forgive them for they know not what they do."

Joseph, wanting to close his eyes and not finish watching the life of Jesus coming to a close, started to scream, "Why are they doing this? He has done nothing to them but love, teach and heal them!"

Gabriel answered Joseph, "You are feeling the pains of any father who has loved and lost a child. Your Heavenly Father, Jesus' Father, feels even greater agony than thou. He has the power and the willing service of 12 legions of angels ready to destroy the wicked and save Jesus from the cross. He only needs to give the word, but He does not. And praise be to the Father forever for not succumbing to his anguish and pain and allowing Jesus to complete his mission. Thereby He will give us our Savior and Redeemer for all to worship and glorify for all eternity."

Joseph seeing the horror unfold in front of him watched as Jesus died on the cross.

The vision came to a close and Gabriel still stood in front of Joseph and said, "Joseph, this is how salvation is to come to the world."

Joseph, trying to gain his composure and dry his face, then asked, "Please, if you will, allow me to inquire further."

"As you wish," Gabriel said.

"When Jesus was on the cross I saw Mary there. But I was not. Why was I not there? For I know for certain that I would be by his side." Joseph asked.

Gabriel looked at Joseph compassionately and said, "For this cause was I sent to show you these things. What I am about to tell you, you shall tell no man.

"Joseph, your years on this earth are numbered and they will end before Jesus starts his ministry. You have seen this so that you might know how to teach Jesus fully. Teach him to be kind, obedient, merciful, just, humble, loyal, courageous, and reverent, full of charity and truth. Do all of this by example so he may look to see what manner of man he must become. Don't let a day go by without showing how much you care for him and love him. Show your love for Mary his mother that he may know how women should be respected and adored."

"To this end were you chosen; now, with soberness I must to speak to you further. You must awake and make haste, for Herod has sent out a decree to kill all male babies under two years old in Bethlehem. Gather a few provisions and take Mary and Jesus and flee to Egypt until I bring you word that Herod has died." Gabriel made an end of speaking and the vision ended.

Joseph quickly awakened and saw that his pillow was soaked with his tears. He heard noise from outside. He went quickly to the window and looked out. He could see torches being carried by Roman soldiers breaking into homes close by. He heard screams of horror from women and men as their sons were brutally murdered. Joseph knew that it was only a matter of minutes before the soldiers would be at their door. He ran to the bedroom.

"Mary you must get up," Joseph said with alarm.

"What is it Joseph?" Mary asked.

"Get Jesus, clothes and provisions that we can carry on our backs, and prepare to leave at once," Joseph said as he ran to blow out any light source in the house.

"Why are we doing this? What is going on?"

"Mary, an angel has appeared to me in a dream and has told me that Herod has released a terrible decree because he fears that Jesus threatens his rule. He has ordered that all male children two years and younger are to be killed. We need to flee to Egypt. Do not wait any longer, we must go," Joseph explained as quickly as he could.

Just then Mary heard the screams of houses just down their street. Mary leaped out of bed, grabbed Jesus, clothes and provisions as Joseph plotted their escape.

"Mary we will sneak out the back. Keep in the alley ways until we reach the East Gate. There we will make our escape to Jerusalem to get better prepared for our journey to Egypt," Joseph explained.

"Joseph, I am scared. What if they catch us?" Mary said in fear.

Joseph took Mary by the hand and said, "God is not going to forsake us. He will prepare a way. I know it," Joseph said kindly, to squelch Mary's fears.

Joseph led the way as they quietly exited out their back door only to hear soldiers coming around the side of their house. Joseph rushed Mary to the other side of the house, kneeling down so they were not as easy to spot.

The soldiers kicked down their back door and rushed inside. While the soldiers were out of view Joseph led Mary to the front of the house, then they quickly ran down the maze of alley ways toward the gate.

They were almost there when they saw and heard soldiers coming down the alley. Although Joseph wanted to stay in the alley he knew if they did they would be caught. Joseph, not having another option, took Mary out to the wide street where they could be spotted easily.

There were soldiers everywhere. Joseph had never seen such an army. Everywhere there were screams of anguish. Parents and children were being slaughtered in almost every house.

In that moment his worst fear came true. There were soldiers coming towards them from both directions carrying torches and blood stained swords. And there was nowhere to hide.

"Joseph, what are we going to do?" Mary said, frightened and shaking.

To make matters worse a goat tied up close to them began making noise and drawing attention.

Then Joseph got an idea. Next to the goat was a rain barrel that was empty. He took Jesus from Mary and placed him in the barrel. Then he took out his knife and slit the throat of the goat with one swooping motion. Warm blood rushed all over his hands. He took the blood and smeared it all over the front of his clothes. He then dipped his hand in more blood and started covering Mary's clothes and said, "Mary, huddle over the goat and start screaming," Joseph demanded.

"They will catch us," Mary said.

"Just do this, it is our only hope," Joseph snapped back.

And with that Mary started to scream and yell very loudly. Joseph huddled around Mary and started to cry as well. Yelling, "Why did they kill our son, why?" He kept repeating this over and over.

The soldiers saw two parents covered in blood huddling over what they thought was a dead child, but in reality it was the goat. Jesus at this point, not knowing what was going on, started to cry as well. But his cries were muffled as Joseph and Mary wailed louder.

The soldiers stopped and looked at Mary and Joseph and then continued on. After the soldiers were further down the road, Joseph took Jesus in one arm, and Mary by the hand, and ran to the next alley way.

Not hearing the screams of Mary and Joseph any longer, one of the soldiers looked back, and saw they were gone. He ran back to where they had been. When he reached the place he saw the dead goat and called for his comrades to return.

The other soldiers turned and started running back toward their comrade. By the time they returned and got organized to search it was too late.

Joseph and Mary had made their escape and were outside the walls of Bethlehem.

....

That night Joseph and Mary slept in the same cave where Jesus had been born and waited until morning. Then they put on fresh clothes and burned the clothes stained with blood.

They could still hear the mourning of the people in Bethlehem. Their hearts went out to them, knowing that the families perished that night because of Herod's perverse ruthlessness.

"I wish this night could be erased from my mind," Mary said, tears starting to well up in her eyes again.

Joseph took Mary and Jesus and guided them towards Jerusalem to quickly buy supplies and make their way to Egypt. For he knew that as long as Herod was alive he would not stop until they were all dead.

On their journey to Egypt Joseph looked up to the sky and said in his mind, "Father, thank you for your protection and sending us warning. I am forever your humble servant and will raise your Son with your direction and guidance to prepare him to fulfill his wonderful mission as the Messiah, Savior to the world."

After thinking these thoughts these words came to his mind 'My son Joseph, I am always with you even to the end. You will be blessed and recorded in history. Stay diligent in keeping my commandments and all will be well with you. And Joseph, for all the things that you have undertaken in keeping my Only Begotten safe: Well done!'

THE END

Chapter Notes

Notes from Chapter 3

Very little is known about how Joseph discovered Mary's pregnancy, we just know that the real reason for her pregnancy was revealed after Mary was found to be with child. We also don't know the timing in which Joseph found out and when Mary left for Elisabeth's home the scriptures only tell us that she went in haste.

We also don't know much about Joseph's immediate family. The author has taken liberties with these unknowns and filled them in with imaginative narrative of how things might of unfolded and the bewilderment that Joseph must of felt between coming across the information of Mary and finding out the truth. We can also imagine the feelings of Joseph's father and mother and trying to protect their child from a situation that could prove to affect the rest of his life.

....

The hatred between Samaritans and the Jews was very intense at this time. The author's research showed that their differences stem from the separation of the Jews between the Northern and Southern Jewish kingdoms that happened during the Babylon exile. The Northern King built the strong defensive city of Samaria. This City controlled the valley, which the main road ran from Jerusalem to Galilee. The city eventually fell into the hands of the Assyrians and became the province of Samarina. Since many inhabitants were led away captive some of them were left behind as farmers and they intermarried with new people from Mesopotamia and Syria.

Later when the Jews from the Northern Kingdom returned from exile, the Samaritans were ready to welcome them back, however the returning Jews despised the Samaritans because of their inter-marital practices. The Samaritans later offered to help in rebuilding the Temple in Jerusalem but there help was rejected. This rejection caused political hostility and opposition, which caused retribution from the Samaritans by undermining the Jews and slowing the rebuilding of Jerusalem and its temple.

Later a son of a High Priest married a daughter of a Syrian governor and then son and his new bride were driven out of Jerusalem for defiling the priesthood by marrying a non-Jew. The governor of Syria then had a temple built in which his new son-in-law could function and this is when the full break between the Jews and Samaritans took place.

The fact that there was such dislike and hostility between Jews and Samaritans is what gives the use of the Samaritan in the Parable of the Good Samaritan (Luke 10:29-37) such strength! The Samaritan is the one who is able to rise above centuries of bigotry and prejudices and show mercy and compassion for the injured Jew after the Jew's own country-men pass him by.

Notes from Chapter 4

The author has made an assumption as to the age of Mary at the time of the angel Gabriel's visit. Since a lot of girls at this time were married at the age of 15, almost all girls were married at least by 16 and there were very few that did not get married. So the author took the oldest probable age for Mary and chose it for this narrative.

Travel to Hebron was not an easy journey to make and safety was a huge concern. Of course a young girl could not take this journey alone, but there seemed to always be caravans or parties that were going from the Galilee to Jerusalem, Mary would more than likely joined one of those companies. It was also more than likely that she would have traveled on a donkey as this was the preferred animal for travel among the Jews. Soldiers often accompanied these caravans to assure safe passage from the thieves and robbers that hid along the way to spring on unwise travelers traveling in small groups or alone.

....

One would think that Mary would have turned to her mother or grandmother for advice and solace in her circumstance, but little is known about her extended family situation. If her mother was living Mary may have felt unsure of her mother or father's response or even that of her grandparents to the announcement of the divine events that were unfolding. Due to the fact that the Gabriel told Mary that Elisabeth, her cousin was expecting she may have felt an extra connection and understanding with her.

Therefore it may make sense for her to make such an extensive journey to be with Elisabeth.

Notes from Chapter 5

There are two thoughts on how Joseph discovered Mary's pregnancy and then resolved to divorce her. One is that of suspicion, he thought that Mary was unfaithful and therefore not wanting to make a spectacle of her desired to divorce her quietly. Another is that Joseph knew that the baby Mary was carrying was of God and he felt inadequate or unworthy of such a task and therefore wanted to divorce himself from that task.

It made sense to the author that it is possible that both scenarios could have occurred. Once Joseph came to grips with what he was chosen to do he 'stepped up to the plate', so to speak and performed his role as the earthly father to Jesus. This hesitancy to perform ones calling based on feelings of inadequacy is not uncommon in scripture. Moses and Jeremiah both felt inadequate, but later were given the help they needed from heaven to fulfill all that was asked and required of them.

These two examples were given in this chapter to try and show why Joseph may have had second thoughts. The only thing we know for sure is the conversation that took place between Joseph and Gabriel which was given in Matthew chapter 1:20. There was no mention of any other conversation that took place. Other conversations in this chapter, how the vision appeared with the exception of what is given in the scriptures in speculation based on feelings of the author. All we know is Joseph had a dream in which he was told of the divine conception and future birth of our Savior. The rest is given to aid the reader in understanding the importance of what Joseph was asked to do and why it was him that was chosen.

Notes from Chapter 9

We know from Luke's account that when Mary came to see Elisabeth that her baby (John the Baptist) leaped in her womb. This was probably more than just an ordinary kick, but something more significant. We also know that Elisabeth had it revealed to her regarding Mary's pregnancy with Jesus to which she prophesied, being full of the Holy Ghost.

In the chapter there was also quotes taken out of Luke 1: 10 – 26 regarding Elisabeth's husband Zacharias and his dealings with an angel in the temple. Everything outside of what is quoted in these verses is narrative from the author.

We don't know when Mary and Joseph met to discuss wedding plans. In 'Joseph's Story' the author had Joseph travel to Hebron to see Mary, because it made sense that any man in love would go to great lengths to help their fiancé in any time of need or concern. Rules were pretty strict with couples being alone together outside of being married. It was not appropriate and a chaperone would be necessary anytime a betrothed or courting couple wanted to see each other.

....

There are some traditions that say that upon Herod's decree to kill all male children of Bethlehem younger that two years of age that Zacharias was killed in the temple because he would not reveal the whereabouts of his son John (John the Baptist). Though Mathews account signifies that the massacre happened in Bethlehem, it is not known why this might have been spread to Jerusalem and affected Zacharias and his family.

Notes from Chapter 10

This story mentions many times and in many places situations regarding the 'zealot movement' which started in the 1ˢᵗ century. The zealots were a group of people wanting to rebel against the Roman Empire with force to drive them out of their land. They tried to incite their country-men to join them. To accomplish their goals they resorted to what some may consider terrorism.

They looked forward to a promise that a king would be born, rise up and take them to victory. They obviously misinterpreted the scriptures regarding the savior. The government that would be on his shoulders would be his heavenly government and the kingdom that would never end would be his heavenly kingdom.

The author used this movement as an element of the story to show the strong disturbance between the Romans and the Jews.

Notes from Chapter 16

The traditional Christmas story portrays a Mary and Joseph traveling alone to Bethlehem, where it would not have been wise for them to do so. The author used circumstances in this chapter to show characteristics of Joseph and how bold and courageous Joseph must have been to protect Mary and the unborn Jesus. The author included the fight between Lucius and Joseph to signify another waging battle, one between heaven and earth, and that angels in heaven played an active role to thwart the adversary's attempts to stop Jesus' birth from taking place.

Notes from Chapter 17

The more common Christmas tradition states that Mary was in labor when she and Joseph arrived in Bethlehem and delivered Jesus in a stable where he was laid in a manger because there was no room for them in the inn.

Some think otherwise; due to the Greek word 'kataluma', which is the word that was translated into the word 'inn'. Kataluma has multiple meanings and could be interpreted as 'guest room' or a room within a private home and that Jesus was laid in a manger (feeding trough of animals) because there was no room for a crib in the 'guest room'. This discrepancy is because Jesus had his last supper in a 'kataluma' or an upper room of a private home.

There was no mention of a cave or stable in the scriptures, but it was assumed such since that is where one would most likely find a manger. Excavations in that area have shown domestic stables built into homes, where animals could be kept inside during the night.

It is also fact that some people had an ancestral home where relatives could stay when traveling to their home cities. There might have been others in their family who arrived prior to Joseph and Mary and the only room available would be downstairs near the animal stable. Therefore there is a thought that Jesus was born in a home of Joseph's relatives and then laid in a manger, that was already inside the home, because there was no room for a crib in the 'guest room'. In 'Joseph's Story' the author chose to keep with the traditional understanding of where Christ was born and took excerpts found in the book of Luke.

The scene of an angelic visit to the shepherds of Christ's birth was taken from Luke chapter 2:10-14.

Notes from Chapter 18

This chapter includes Joseph and Mary's visit to the temple where they brought Jesus to be given a name, blessed and circumcised. This account can be found in Luke 2:25-34.

It also gives an account of the visit of the wise men (magi) from the East. It is assumed that there were three because there were three gifts given to Jesus. In the East, the usual number for Magi is twelve.

The three gifts, however were significant. In the Old Testament the Queen of Sheba visited King Solomon and brought him Gold and spices. Gold and Frankincense are *rare, valuable and precious commodities. These items represent the best to be offered from different parts of the world. Since these visitor recognized Jesus as a King, it makes sense that they would give these most precious and rare items. These gifts were reserved for only the highest of honors.*

Frankincense is a sweet smelling sap, which hardens and then used for incense or for perfume. Frankincense was burned as incense in the temple because of its rare, wonderful smell.

Myrrh is also sweet smelling sap from a tree, but its uses are quite different from Frankincense. The most practical uses for Joseph and Mary would most likely be its medical uses as an ointment.

Notes from Chapter 19

This was a hard chapter to write for two reasons. One, it was hard to create the utter ruthlessness of Herod to help the reader comprehend how he could make such an order to kill all male children under the age of two. The horror of that time must have been awful in ways words cannot describe.

Two, this chapter recounts a quick narrative of the atonement of the savior, which Christ's appeal to the Father in Gethsemane to take the cup from him if possible and when he was on the cross pleading to forgive those who were crucifying him. I tried to bring a spirit of awe to what the savior went through for us. These few paragraphs are the apex to our fathers plan. I can only imagine the agony of both our Father in Heaven and Christ in these moments. One can imagine all of their creations crying for justice and wanting to save Jesus from his tormenters. It is impossible to describe what it would have been like.

Quotes were taken from Luke chapters 22-23.